To the faculty of
Bryan College
with sincere appreciation
for your help in
shaping my spiritual
life

Pai Ye Toha

(an alumnus)

1979

EVERETT BOYCE

The Chinese Connection

The Chinese Connection

Pai Ye Loh

貝 仁 樂

(Everett R. Boyce)

Fleming H. Revell Company
Old Tappan, New Jersey

Unless otherwise identified Scripture quotations are based on the King James Version of the Bible.

Scripture quotation identified NEB is from The New English Bible. © The Delegates of the Oxford University Press and the Syndics of the Cambridge University Press 1961 and 1970. Reprinted by permission.

> This story is based on the true experiences of those who have dared to invade the People's Republic of China for the cause of Christ. In some cases, the names have been changed.

Library of Congress Cataloging in Publication Data

Loh, Pai Ye.
    The Chinese connection.

    I. Title.
PZ4.L836Ch [PS3562.0458]   813'.5'4   78-16880
ISBN 0-8007-0954-3

Brother Andrew has proved that there are no closed countries. His challenge to obey the great commission has motivated many to serve the suffering Church.

Brother David's single-minded dedication to the Christians in the People's Republic of China has inspired many overseas Chinese to dare to seek out and serve the suffering Christians in that great country.

To these two great saints of God this book is lovingly dedicated.

Contents

Foreword

This story by Pai Ye Loh is impressive, because it is so real. Oh, it is fiction; but it reflects accurately the truth of China as I know it.

I have traveled in China, as I know the author has, many times. I've talked with Chinese young people, both from the Mainland and from among overseas Chinese families. They experience all the tensions and conflicting claims on their loyalties—and many of them are doing what Lee Kai-chang did—sacrificing their all to make a difference.

It might seem preposterous, in the face of a monolithic, closed society such as that controlling Red China's 800,000,000 people, to think that a single life can make a difference. But if we recognize the nature of the struggle as a spiritual one, then you know you can help the cause of Christ in China to the degree you are willing to care, to learn, to suffer, to give, and to go.

Young people in a rally in Peking carried a banner with the slogan, "Go Where the Revolution Needs You Most!" That should be the challenge every Christian is ready to accept: "Go Where the Kingdom Needs You Most!"

I know many young Chinese Christians who are going into China regularly, along with the one million other visitors who come and go from that country every year. They run a risk—they might not come back. But they have told me, "It is easy to get into China if you are willing not to come out again."

9

Perhaps that is what makes *The Chinese Connection* so real to me. It is based on that kind of dedication of life. We need to learn that, for only as we are willing to embrace a position that extreme, only when we are willing for *anything* in order to serve our Lord, only then will China be won for Christ.

                                              BROTHER ANDREW

1 Raid on the Police Station

Somewhere in Taiwan

The group worked quickly and quietly. They knew exactly what was expected of them. Lee was so excited he could hardly make his nervous fingers behave. He'd just about finished making the Molotov cocktails when Toto spoke.

"Is everyone ready?" Toto peered at each one of them in the dim light.

Each one nodded, eyeing Toto intently.

"Very well, then," he replied. "Let's load up."

Lee had already decided that he wanted to ride on the back of the jeep. It would be the best place for him to keep his throwing arm free. Since this was his first chance to be in an attack squad, he wanted Toto to notice him. He took the old rifle they had given him and laid it on the floor of the jeep. With four men and two girls in the vehicle, there wouldn't be any room to use it up there, anyway. He straddled the back, his left leg inside and his right foot braced against the bumper. That way he could hold one firebomb in each hand and quickly switch from one hand to the other to throw.

When everyone was settled and quiet, Toto swung open the front doors. They sat absolutely still for several minutes until a light flashed twice a short distance down the road.

The jeep engine roared to life and they lurched out into the road, turned a hard left, and raced toward the village. Lee found that he had a harder time just hanging on than he had anticipated.

Toto turned right for a short distance, then turned right again. Suddenly they were almost in front of the police station. Toto jumped the jeep up onto the wide sidewalk so that they could get as close as possible to the front door.

Two policemen came out the door just as they roared up onto the sidewalk. The policemen stood motionless for an instant, staring at the onrushing vehicle, then quickly turned to run back into the station.

But they were too late. The girl in the right front seat cut them down with a long burst of fire from her submachine gun. In the seconds it took to flash past the station door, someone on the left fired a steady stream of ammunition into the line of police cars and jeeps parked at the curb. At the same time, Lee and two others were heaving grenades and firebombs at the front door.

Lee saw his first throw burst harmlessly against the stone wall, but the second sailed accurately through the gaping doorway where a grenade had blown the door off the hinges.

Lee cheered loudly. This was more fun than skydiving and auto racing combined. As the jeep jumped off the curb and raced down the road, men began to pour out of the station into the street. Toto weaved the jeep from side to side, trying to avoid their fire until they reached the next corner. Just before Toto turned sharply into the side street, Lee began to climb over the back into the jeep.

Suddenly he felt a sharp blow to his back. The impact pitched him onto his face on the floor, on top of the old rifle. He lay there for some time, trying to comprehend what had happened. At first he thought one of the other men had struck him, but that didn't make sense. Eventually he realized he'd been shot although, strangely enough, he couldn't feel anything.

He heard Toto ask, "How did we do?"

"The building was burning when we turned the corner," someone replied. "I think Lee got one right inside."

"Any casualties?" Toto demanded.

"Kim is dead. Took a shot in the head. Lee may be gone, too."

Lee tried to raise himself up to protest, but he felt the blackness closing in around him. The voices seemed to go farther and farther away as he drifted down into the dark void. Faintly, as though in the distance, he heard someone say, "We can't do anything for him. Just leave him and let's go."

"We can't leave him alive. They can have Kim, but I'm not going to leave them a live one."

That was Toto's voice, Lee thought.

The first voice, a female voice, spoke again—more clearly this time. "Then let's finish him. They will be here soon. He can't live with that hole in him, anyway."

"No," he heard Toto say. "I think he can make it. The wound is above the heart and the lungs. Maybe we could take him somewhere and call his parents. They could get him home."

Lee still wasn't sure whether or not his eyes were open, but he made a concentrated effort to speak.

"Did he say something?" Toto asked.

"Just a groan," the girl answered.

Lee forced himself to try again. "N—no," he mumbled faintly.

"I'm sure he said something," Toto said. "It sounded like he said 'no.' "

"I think he's dying," she insisted.

Lee strained with all his strength, slowly forcing the words, "Not—home—take me with you—" Then he lost consciousness again. For a time there was nothing but blackness interrupted by periods of blinding, searing pain. Then blackness again.

Much later the blackness turned to gray and he became aware of sounds—soft, peaceful sounds. A jungle bird, someone pounding rice, rain dripping from the roof. He lay half conscious, enjoying the pleasant, comforting noises for a long time.

He felt the bamboo slats of the floor moving gently under him and realized that someone was squatting at his side. His eyelids were glued shut. He moved his right hand slowly away from his body until he touched a bare foot. He felt the foot gently, hesitantly—then the leg.

"If that isn't a typical playboy," a female voice said. "Feeling a girl's leg before he even says hello." The voice cut through the haze and he forced his eyes open. A young, attractive girl was smiling at him.

"Wh—who are you?" he asked haltingly.

"I'm your nurse, and it begins to look as though you might make it. Are you—" Her voice trailed off as the gray mist descended around him and he again lost consciousness.

The next time he became aware of his surroundings, the room was quiet. He opened his eyes and surveyed as much as he could of the place without moving his head. Instinctively he knew that moving his head would hurt.

He was in a peasant hut with slat bamboo walls and floor and a thatched roof. There was no furniture. He closed his eyes again and was conscious that someone had come up the ladder into the hut. He opened his eyes just enough to see the young girl squatting on the other side of the room, cleaning a submachine gun. Her dark hair was closely cropped, giving her a boyish appearance which was in turn belied by the soft curves of her body. Her small, well-shaped hands moved deftly, expertly. Lee recognized her at once as the one who'd shot the policeman in the raid.

"You really cut them down," he said.

"What?" Startled, she raised her eyes. He was surprised to

find that instead of being dark, they were tawny and gold-flecked. "You're back, are you?" she observed. "What did you say?"

"You really cut them down," he repeated.

"What are you talking about?"

"Those policemen, in that last raid," he said. He felt his forehead break out with perspiration. Just talking was an effort.

She laid the gun aside and walked over to him. Kneeling beside him, she brushed her hand across his forehead and smiled at him, showing a row of small, even, white teeth against the background of her olive skin.

"That raid was quite a while ago," she said. "We've had another one and have ambushed a patrol since then. Are you hungry?"

He frowned, confused. It was so hard to concentrate. He felt that he was losing consciousness again. "Not—now—" he managed to say. As he drifted off, he was faintly aware of her hand stroking his cheek.

When he finally awoke again, he was very hungry. He looked around the room, hoping to see the girl. Although the room was empty, he could hear someone outside, so he whistled softly. He wasn't sure yet just where he was, but he knew that his presence here might be a secret. He was a little disappointed when an elderly woman entered the hut and came over to his side. She was small and frail with white hair and dark skin, leathery from years of exposure to the elements.

"Good morning, sir," she said, using the old-fashioned form of respect that the peasants used when addressing the upper class. "You are looking much better today."

"I feel better, thank you," Lee replied. Then he asked, "Where is the young lady who was here?"

"She will be here later. She comes every day to check on you. At first she stayed right with you for three days. We all thought you would die." She bent over and straightened his bandages. "Not that your wound was so bad," she added.

"The bullet did not hit anything too important, but you lost much blood. Both Cheetah and Toto were covered with blood by the time they got you here."

"Cheetah?" he inquired.

"The young lady you asked about. Don't you know her?"

So that's her name, he thought. *Appropriate. The way she looks and moves, she is very much like a cheetah.*

"I—uh—I've seen her a couple of times, but I do not know her well," he said casually.

The old woman nodded. "She certainly has taken care of you. I thought perhaps she was your sister." She gave a little laugh, adding, "or something."

Lee ignored the innuendo. "Tell me, where am I?" he asked.

"This is my little home," she said, smiling shyly, "thanks to Captain Toto. My husband and I lived in the valley all our lives. We tenants farmed some rice land that his father and his grandfather had worked before him. Then our landlord decided to sell the land for a factory. He told us we would have to leave. But we had no place to go. Farming was all we knew." She took a deep breath and continued resolutely. "My husband pleaded with the landlord, but he just laughed. When the men came to put us off, my husband tried to stop them. He even threatened them with his knife. But he was an old man. They just laughed at him. When he really tried to hit one of them, they shot him. He was still alive when they took him away. I never saw him again. They told me he died," she added, her voice barely a whisper.

"How did Toto help you?" Lee asked.

"He heard about it somehow. He found me in an alley. I was living on food scraps that a restaurant was throwing away. He brought me up here and built this hut. He and his men helped me to plant the rice. Toto says that they had no right to take our land."

Lee nodded.

"Let me get you some soup," she said. She went outside

and came back a short time later with a steaming bowl. Kneeling beside Lee on the rice mat, she patiently held the bowl to his lips until it was all gone. Then, having made him comfortable, she disappeared.

Later Cheetah came back. Lee heard footsteps and felt the hut move. He lay with his eyes closed, hoping it would be Cheetah. Coming to his side, she knelt down and touched his cheek. He reached for her hand, slowly opening his eyes.

"I've missed you," he said.

She laughed. "Until today you didn't know whether I was here or not. Lo Wan says you have eaten well."

"Last time I woke up, I was very hungry." He paused and looked at her for a long moment. "Lo Wan brought me some soup. But I really wanted to see you."

She squeezed his hand, then said lightly, "You playboys are all alike. You sweet-talk the girls every chance you get."

"Don't call me that," he said. "I joined Toto just to prove I'm not a playboy."

She smiled, raising her eyebrows and giving her slim shoulders a slight shrug. "We can talk about that later," she replied.

Lee remained serious. "Cheetah," he said softly, "I've liked you from the first time I saw you."

She pulled her hand away and stood over him, scoffing, "You tried to seduce me the first time you saw me! You were barely conscious and you didn't even know my name. As I said before, you playboys are all alike." Turning, she walked toward the doorway and lit a kerosene lamp against the growing dusk.

She does remind me of a cheetah, he thought, not for the first time. *The way she moves—so gracefully, so stealthily.*

"But we will get to know each other well in the weeks ahead," she said, turning to face him. At these words he felt a sudden surge of excitement. But his smile froze on his face as she added, "Toto says that I am to reeducate you and make a true communist of you."

2 Recovery and Indoctrination

Lee regained his strength rapidly after he began eating regularly. Cheetah continued to stop by occasionally to see him, but her visits were brief and businesslike. Before much time had passed, Lee became bored and, as he felt his strength returning, he began to take walks farther and farther from the hut. It was evident that they were deep in a rugged part of the jungle. As far as Lee walked, he never saw anyone else. In due time he determined the most likely route back toward town and began to consider the possibility of leaving.

Although his left arm and shoulder remained very stiff and painful, he began to do simple calisthenics. He had always been very athletic, and his present weakness was a blow to his pride.

Cheetah came to the hut one day when he was doing his exercises. He didn't realize she was watching from the edge of the clearing until she spoke.

"Excellent, comrade. The more quickly you regain your strength, the sooner you can return to the struggle."

"Oh, hello," he said in surprise. "I didn't hear you coming."

"You were not supposed to," she replied casually. "Go ahead. Don't let me interrupt you."

He continued, grinning. "Do you do exercises?"

She shook her head and shrugged nonchalantly, but Lee pursued the point. "I thought you must. You're in such beautiful physical condition."

Cheetah ignored the implication. "The only proper purpose for that sort of thing is as you are using it—to recover from illness or injury," she commented.

"But," he protested, "many healthy people exercise every day just to stay in good physical condition."

Cheetah dismissed his opinion with a desultory wave of her hand. "That sort of exercise," she announced emphatically, "is the plaything of the idle rich. The working man does not need it. It is the province of the decadent bourgeoisie."

Lee railed inwardly. "I didn't mean to push your party-ideology button," he said. "I was only making conversation."

Cheetah did not appreciate his mild sarcasm. To her, party ideology was not a joking matter. "You have much to learn about the proletariat," she replied quickly. "We do not even converse about the same things as do the bourgeoisie." She sat down, pulling her knees up in front of her. Her tawny eyes glittered shrewdly as she surveyed Lee critically for a moment. Then, resting her head on her knees, she went on. "For example, you think it strange that I have been assigned to teach you, don't you?"

Lee stopped his exercises and wiped the perspiration from his face. He didn't know what to say. He studied Cheetah thoughtfully for a moment. It was obvious that Toto considered this girl to be something special. He had assumed it was just because she was an attractive female. But maybe there was even more to Cheetah than met the eye. Leaning against a tree and appraising her with interest, he replied, "I have wondered how much education you have had."

She gave him a brief, condescending smile. "I can read and write. I went to school part of several years until the second year of secondary school. And you?"

Lee was suddenly uncomfortable. "Ah, well—I got a little more than that," he stammered.

"You graduated from an exclusive private primary and secondary school," she snapped, "and from the state university with a degree in business administration—in spite of all your playboy escapades!"

Lee was on the defensive with her and he didn't like it. "Since you know so much about me," he countered, "why did you ask?"

"Because I wanted to get it out in the open," she retorted. "You have a typical bourgeois education. You have learned to propagate your opinions, your class, and your life-style. All you know about the working man is how to manage him." She stopped, looked at him for a long moment, then continued. "Well, I am the proletariat. I have spent a lifetime being reminded of that fact. My father died in a mine accident when I was two. My older sister and I grew up in the streets, living out of garbage cans. My mother married again a few years later, but the man wouldn't have my sister and me. We didn't care because we hated him anyway. He always drank. He would beat my mother every time he got drunk."

Lee interrupted. "And you blame that on the bourgeoisie?"

"Yes!" she fairly shouted. "The poor drink because they hate their lives and they hate themselves. They have been taught that if they really tried, they could improve their lot. But they can't, and they hate themselves for it."

Lee shrugged, but remained silent. Cheetah continued.

"Finally my sister got a job working for some rich people. I thought we were in heaven. We lived there for three years. It was comfortable and clean, and we had plenty to eat."

"Chalk up one for the rich people," Lee commented dryly.

"Wrong!" she snapped. "I later learned that my sister had to sleep with the 'master' "—she spat out the title with distaste— "to keep the job. Finally she decided that if she had to do that, she could make more money as a full-time prostitute. She was then fifteen years old. Of course I had to move out, too. So I went my own way. I became a part-time street vendor and a full-time petty thief. I have stolen everything you can think of."

"I know what you mean," Lee said with sudden compassion. "I have seen teenagers working the streets like that. But they are usually boys."

"I dressed as a boy. I was slim enough to get away with it and a fast enough runner to avoid most fights. Then, when I was sixteen—" her voice trailed off.

Lee waited. At last she took a deep breath and continued, her voice barely audible. "When I was sixteen I got caught stealing a man's watch. Usually they wouldn't chase you very far, but this one kept after me. Finally I couldn't run any more and he caught me. He took his watch back and turned me over to a policeman. He didn't even know I was a girl, and neither did the policeman until he told me to strip at the police station. I refused, so he tore my shirt off.

"As soon as he realized I was female, he covered me up and took me to the judge. He whispered something to the judge and then he took me to a small room. Then the judge came in and they—they both—" Her voice faltered, but her eyes finished the sentence.

The hardness had gone out of her face and she looked very vulnerable. Lee listened quietly, a feeling of compassion stirring inside him, but he said nothing. After a long pause she went on, her voice once again strong.

"So I came to the hills and joined the rebels. They treated me decently. They accepted me as an equal—a fighter. And I have killed more policemen than any of the others!"

"They did not abuse you?" Lee asked.

"Never!" she declared vehemently. "Not a one of them has ever treated me as did the bourgeois dogs!"

Lee could not help insisting, "Not even Toto?"

Her sharp eyes snapped as she stared him down. "Not even Toto. Toto didn't force me. I gave myself to him. I will be his as long as he lives. Don't you forget it!"

Lee squirmed uncomfortably. Cheetah stood up. "That was lesson number one, Comrade Lee. Now you know why I am your teacher. You must learn to think as does the proletariat. Sometimes I wonder if it is really possible, but Chairman Mao says it is, so I must accept it. You will read the books I have left at the hut. When I come again, we will discuss them. I expect you to know their contents thoroughly. Good-bye."

She turned and walked away into the jungle. Lee sat for a long time in deep thought before he turned to the hut and began to study the material Cheetah had brought him.

The next few weeks passed quickly. Cheetah moved into the hut and the two of them were together constantly. She was a surprisingly good teacher. She mixed lessons in theory with sessions in hand-to-hand combat and taught him the techniques of bomb making.

In one of their first theory lessons Lee made the mistake of commenting that theory was dry and unimportant. Cheetah laid the book aside, stood up, and faced him squarely with her small hands planted firmly on her hips.

"Theory is the absolutely indispensable basis for action," she retorted hotly. "People act on what they believe, whether they have thought it through or not. If you want to change people's actions, you must first change their beliefs. Chairman Mao said, 'Communism is at once a complete system of pro-letarian ideology and a new social system. It is different from any other ideological and social system, and it is the most complete, progressive, revolutionary and rational system in human history.' "

Lee sat looking at her and shaking his head.

"You do not accept Chairman Mao's teachings?" she fairly screamed at him.

"No—no, that is not what I mean," he protested. "Of course I accept the thoughts of the great teacher."

She settled down and he went on. "I'm just amazed at you. You quote Mao or Lenin or Marx as readily as most people repeat the alphabet or the multiplication tables."

She relaxed and smiled. "Thank you. That is the greatest compliment anyone has ever given me."

"You are an amazing woman," he added, meaning it.

She stiffened, almost imperceptibly. "Don't spoil everything now," she warned. "Let's get on with the lesson."

She made Lee explain the contents of the books on Marx, Lenin, and Mao that she had given him. Then she asked questions to see if he really understood. He enjoyed the challenge and was constantly amazed at her grasp of the theoretical aspects of communism.

Most of all, however, he enjoyed her company. She could be so much fun at times. They often laughed together and just enjoyed being with each other. And sometimes, when her thoughts were distracted from party ideology, Lee detected a quiet wistfulness about her that he found faintly disturbing. It was as though he'd probed an untouched void in her makeup, and he often wondered if she found her beliefs in communism as fulfilling as she apparently wanted him to think.

But then she would turn hard so suddenly that he was often caught by surprise. At such times it was easy for him to believe that she was a completely dedicated communist. Not once did she evidence an appreciation of his frequent jokes about her commitment. Lee found this perplexing because, despite his indoctrination, he just could not bring himself to take communism seriously. He faithfully memorized the quotes from Chairman Mao's little red book and he knew all the right answers, but he wasn't really convinced. In his alignment with the rebel troops, Lee had found an effective outlet for his aggressive tendencies and a new opportunity for excitement and adventure. In addition, it afforded him a most satisfying way of rebelling against the stifling traditions of his family—his father's obsession with family pride and respectability and his mother's latest religious kick. In rejecting the values of his family, he'd never stopped to consider the fact that he had no real values of his own. And if at times he recognized within himself an aching void which cried out for fulfillment, he found it more expedient to turn his thoughts to other matters.

One morning while they were involved in a demolitions lesson, Cheetah heard someone coming. They quickly ducked into the underbrush and waited. Soon a young man jogged into the clearing and went straight to the hut. The old woman, Lo Wan, was busy washing clothes. The youth made his way over to her, dropped a roll of paper, and ran back in the same direction.

"Do you know him?" Lee whispered to Cheetah just as soon as the messenger disappeared from sight.

She nodded. "He is one of Commander Susong's men. I don't like the looks of this."

They went to the hut and got the note. Cheetah unrolled it carefully and began to decode it. The message was fairly long. Lee walked over to the spring to get a drink of water while she continued to work on it. When he returned, she was burning the note.

"What is it?" he asked.

"Change of plans," she said, trying to be casual, but Lee could tell that she was upset. "Toto wants us in camp as soon as possible. I suppose," she added with a hint of foreboding, "that school is out."

As they quickly gathered their things Lee was torn by mixed emotions. He'd looked forward to some action, but he had also enjoyed these weeks with Cheetah and hated to see them end.

Lo Wan fed them some rice for lunch. Soon afterward they set out at a fast pace for Toto's camp.

"How far is it?" Lee asked after they'd gone a short distance.

"We won't make it before dark," Cheetah replied.

They walked in silence, saving their breath for the hike. Lee enjoyed watching Cheetah walk ahead of him, surefooted and graceful. Again he realized how she had earned the name Cheetah. She was svelte, lithe, catlike in every way.

Lee let his mind wander idly as the miles and the hours

slipped by. He wondered what his family was doing. They probably thought he was dead by now. Although he and his father had never been very close, he was really sorry about his mother. She would have taken the news of his death very hard. In spite of his total rejection of her religious beliefs, she had always believed that he would be "saved" and accept Christianity as she had.

Cheetah turned suddenly from the trail. So preoccupied was Lee with his own thoughts that he almost bumped into her. They stepped through some underbrush and came into a small, grassy clearing. The sun had already set and it was rapidly getting dark.

"It is late," Cheetah observed. "We'll just stretch out on the grass and sleep, and get moving again at sunup. Lie down here."

Already it was so dark that Lee could hardly make out where she was pointing. It was going to be a very dark night. No moon or stars, only a heavy overcast of clouds. He lay down obediently, wondering what she was going to do. In a few minutes she lay down near him. She felt for his face in the darkness and put her head next to his. He could smell the fragrance of her hair. All those nights in the hut she had never been so close.

"We could talk quietly, if you like," she whispered softly. He turned his face toward her, and his lips brushed her forehead. He hesitated, expecting her to pull away, but she didn't move. At last, Lee put his hand on her head, turned her face slightly, and kissed her gently. She responded. He kissed her again, this time more insistently. Again she responded. He lay back quietly, trying to think. He wanted to move closer to her, but he wasn't sure he dared. He had just about decided to try when she whispered, "Thank you, Lee. Good night."

He felt her roll away, striving for a comfortable position. He turned his back to her and lay there mentally kicking himself for his awkwardness until at last he fell asleep.

It seemed he had hardly slept at all before he heard her

voice rousing him. "Lee—Lee. Wake up. We've got to get going."

The sun was just lighting the sky and the trail was barely visible. Lee didn't see why they had to leave so soon.

"Are we really in that much of a hurry?" he asked, still groggy from sleep.

"Yes," she hissed in his ear. "It could be a matter of life-and-death."

Her remark startled him into complete consciousness and he jumped up quickly. In a few minutes they were ready to go. She headed off at the same rapid pace of the previous day, Lee following close behind.

The sun was high in the sky when at last they stopped on one side of an open valley. Cheetah stood on an outcropping of rock and waved a prearranged signal to an unseen guard somewhere across the valley. Then they resumed their trek. They crossed the valley and had just begun the ascent on the other side when suddenly they were surrounded by four armed men.

"Hello, Cheetah," one of the men said, lowering his gun and pointing it at the ground.

"Why are you stopping us?" she demanded.

"Orders. Toto told us to double-check your companion."

"Does he think I would bring someone else into camp?" she asked in an irritated tone.

"Just a precaution." He turned to Lee. "Turn around and pull up your shirt."

Lee complied, exposing the freshly healed wound in the back of his left shoulder.

"That's fine," the man said, slapping Lee's shoulder in a comradely way. "They really put a hole in you, didn't they?"

Lee nodded abruptly and saluted, as Cheetah hurried on, and jogged to catch up with her. Cheetah didn't waste any time.

"Is this Toto's camp?" he asked, coming alongside her.

Cheetah nodded. They entered a patch of heavy underbrush and went inside a small hut where Toto was kneeling, studying a map.

"Greetings, comrades," he said without looking up.

"Why did you—?" Cheetah started to question him, but he cut her off with a wave of his hand.

"Not now, We will talk later." He turned to Lee. "Commander Susong's band was wiped out four days ago. They had set up an ambush for an army patrol, but it turned out to be a trap. Only Susong and two of his men escaped. Susong was badly wounded. He had his men bring him here."

"That was stupid," Cheetah stated.

Toto nodded in agreement. "Susong died this morning. His men say they lost their pursuers ten kilometers east of here. But if they were trailed across this ridge, it is only a matter of time until they find us."

"Why don't you just move?" Lee asked.

"We have been stockpiling weapons and ammunitions in this area for two years," Toto replied. "When the revolution comes, these will be vital. We must not give them up if we can avoid it."

"Do we have enough men to fight them?"

"No. Not an all-out battle. We must try to harass them in this area," he said, pointing to the map, "and then run down this valley to lead them astray. That's why I sent for you. I need all the men I can get."

"*And* women," Cheetah interjected.

"I always need you, wildcat," Toto retorted, grinning at her. She smiled back at Toto and Lee felt a sudden surge of jealousy. He pretended not to notice her and turned his attention back to Toto.

Toto gave a low whistle and a guard came in. "Add Lee, here, to your group," he told the guard. Then he turned to Lee and stretched out his hand. "Welcome to the People's Liberation Army," he said.

In the days ahead Lee took his turn at guard duty and lay around camp. Time dragged by, but the anticipated government offensive never took place. Lee was restless. He rarely saw Cheetah. She stayed in Toto's hut all the time. Whenever he let himself think about it, his insides would knot up. After he'd been in camp for about a week, Toto sent for him.

"I can't figure out why they are not probing that ridge where they lost the trail," Toto told Lee. "Our scouts say that they have moved north and appear to be looking for us up there. I can't understand how they could be so stupid."

"Good luck for us," Lee said.

"Perhaps," Toto agreed. "But we have got to do something. We can't afford to be bottled up here indefinitely."

Lee nodded. The band was getting restless. They didn't have enough supplies to stay in one place for very long. They lived off the land and there were not enough farms this deep in the jungle to supply them with necessary food.

"And besides," Toto continued, "our friends who are supplying our weapons want to be paid."

"So we need money," Lee observed.

"We need to rob a bank," Cheetah suggested.

Lee nodded. "Not a bad idea. The change of routine from attacks on patrols will throw them off, too. Got any particular bank in mind?"

"Yes," Toto declared. "Your father's."

Lee was stunned at this unexpected turn of events. "That's impossible," he stammered, trying to think what to say next. "It—it's right in the heart of the capital. It has the most sophisticated safe in the country. It can't be done."

"You're undoubtedly right," Cheetah conceded. "It could be done only with a man on the inside."

"A man—" Lee looked from Cheetah to Toto and back. "You want me—?" His question went unfinished.

"That's right," Toto nodded. "You will return home as a repentant son. They will accept you, of course, and put you to work in the bank."

"They know I hate the bank," Lee protested. "I've always refused to work there."

Cheetah smiled. "That is why they will put you there, to teach you a lesson."

"But I can't—" Lee floundered helplessly.

"You can," Toto assured him. "And you must. We are counting on you. Cheetah will accompany you back to the edge of town. She will be your contact. You can work out the details on your way back. It will probably take a few months for you to figure out how we can do it, but get it done as quickly as possible." He slapped the palm of his hand down on the makeshift table for added emphasis.

"But—" Lee stammered, still unable to accept the idea.

"Comrade!" Cheetah snapped. "With the death of Susong, Toto is our commander. He has the entire People's Liberation Army in this country to think about. You will obey!"

Lee nodded.

"Good-bye, comrade," Toto said. "And good luck."

3 Using the Family for the Cause

It was even worse than Lee had expected. He'd known that his grandmother would rebuke him. He had even considered the possibility that she would turn him over to the police. But he hadn't dreamed that she would make such a production out of the whole thing.

The stern matriarch was seated in her favorite chair. Just behind her the wall was decorated with a huge picture of Chiang Kai-shek. Lee stood silently before her and listened with resignation to her seemingly endless harangue, thinking that she must have been practicing her speech all the time he was gone.

He stood motionless, his head bowed. His parents stood behind him, in deference to the woman whose advancing years had freed her from the ignominy of womankind and given her an exalted position in the family. It was hard for them as well. Grandmother was recalling every detail of family history, expressing the conviction that the character weakness she had perceived on his mother's side of the family was to blame for his recent behavior.

Lee knew his mother must be burning inside. She was a

31

dedicated Christian who rarely lost her temper, but this tirade against her family would probably set her off.

Lee's mind wandered as the lecture went on. Everyone in his family identified himself as a Christian, having put aside ancestor worship several generations ago. His mother, however, was the only one who took her religion very seriously, and even that was a fairly recent development. Her younger brother Wang had come under the influence of one of those extremely religious student groups while attending college overseas. Upon returning, he had tried to convert the whole family but she was the only one who had paid much attention.

Lee glanced out of the corner of his eye at his father who stood stoically accepting the rebuke. He stifled a feeling of amusement as he thought of the employees at the bank who would catch the brunt of his father's wrath.

"Do I make myself clear, Lee Kai-chang?" his grandmother asked.

"Yes, Grandmother," Lee stammered, not at all sure what he was agreeing to.

"Very well, then. I expect you to take him to the bank and make a useful worker out of him," she said to his father. "His days of playing are over. My favorite grandson has been away on a long journey, but now he has returned to take his proper place in the family business," she announced to them all.

Then, turning her attention to Lee again, she went on. "But let me make it completely clear, young man, that if there is any further evidence of weakness and lack of loyalty in your character, you shall be held accountable to the Lee family."

Lee nodded dumbly. She dismissed them with a wave of her hand and slumped down in the chair. He was impressed with her display of strength and stamina. He and his parents left the room. In the hall outside the door they faced each other.

Lee's mother was quite obviously livid with rage, but she bit her lower lip momentarily and then said, "I'm sorry about all this, Lee, but I'm glad you're home." She disappeared down the hall.

"Well, I'm not," his father said. "I don't think you got half what you deserve and I'm not glad you're home. If I had my way, you would not have been allowed into the house until you had told us the whole story."

"But, father—" Lee explained, "I told you how I—"

"I don't believe a word of that tale," his father interrupted. "I don't know where you've been or what you've been up to. But I will expect you at the bank in the morning. You can start by sweeping the floors. You have not shown me that you have either the desire or the ability to contribute to the bank. You are granted this opportunity only because your grandmother requested it." With that, he turned and walked away.

Lee smiled. *Since grandmother happens to be chairman of the board and the major stockholder in the bank,* he thought with amusement and mild contempt, *her requests carry a lot of weight.*

He walked slowly to his room. Toto had pretty well figured out how it would go, except it didn't look as though a janitor would be of much help in robbing the bank. He sprawled across the bed. He must conduct himself as the model obedient Chinese son, exactly the role he had always rebelled against. Yet, while living that role, he was dedicated to the overthrow of his family, their whole class, and their puppet government.

He admitted to himself that he felt guilty. Cheetah would tell him, if she knew of his guilt, that he merely needed more education. He didn't really hate his father. He just hated the thought that all his life had to be laid out for him by family traditions and customs. He really wished that things had worked out differently, but he was caught in a web of circumstances beyond his control. He would just have to play out the role and see what happened.

If only Cheetah were here. He had had no contact with her for several days. Then, on Sunday afternoon while everyone else was taking a nap, there was a knock at the door of Lee's bedroom.

He opened the door. "What is it?" he asked the maid who stood in the hall.

The maid seemed nervous. "The street vendor said you wanted these peanuts," she stammered, obviously worried that she would get into trouble for disturbing him at this hour.

"That's fine," Lee assured her. "I do indeed want the peanuts." He reached into his pocket. "Here—give him some money."

"But he said you'd already paid for them," she protested.

"Of course. I quite forgot," he said, closing the door as she hurried away.

This was one of the prearranged ways in which Cheetah was going to contact him. He dumped the contents of the small paper bag onto the bed and turned the bag inside out. In small, faint letters she had penciled the code: 3 + 7/1/16-C-Q. He was to meet her at the corner of the streets they had coded 3 and 7 on Sunday at four o'clock. He should drive a car, and it was to be a secret pickup. Lee waited until about half-past three and then casually strolled to his father's den. He knocked lightly.

"Come in."

He opened the door wide enough to lean his head through and saw his father seated at the desk. His father looked up, expectant.

"I wonder whether you'd mind if I take a little drive in the country," Lee asked.

"I suppose you want to race that sports car around," his father growled.

"No, father," Lee shrugged. "Any one of the cars will do."

"Oh, I don't care," his father said, conceding a point. "I suppose you have earned that much. You made a pretty good janitor." He smiled grudgingly and Lee returned his smile.

Lee had swept the floors only for about two hours. Once the bank opened his father couldn't face the idea of his son being seen doing common janitorial work. Since that time he had been doing odd jobs around the bank but seemed to be spending more and more time in the loan-applications department.

"Go ahead and take the sports car," his father said, tossing Lee the keys. "But stay out of trouble."

Lee took his time, carefully dusting off the handsome sports car in the garage. It had been given to him two years before by his parents. He had enjoyed hours of racing around the country roads near the capital. His mother had hoped that it would satisfy his craving for adventure.

He drove slowly and cautiously to the designated corner, then pulled over near a stand of bushes and got out to check the air pressure in the rear tires. Out of the corner of his eye he saw a figure dart out of the bushes and slip into the space behind the seats. He knew it was Cheetah. He got back into the car and drove several kilometers before speaking.

"Hello, Cheetah," he said at last.

"I go by the name of Sylvia in town," she said, raising her head above the seat. "Sylvia Chung. You can pull over now and I'll get in the front."

As she sat next to him, Lee was surprised at the change in her appearance. She reminded him of a schoolgirl.

"You are a very pretty young lady," Lee declared with exaggerated politeness. "I am happy to take you for a drive in the country."

"Thank you, kind sir," she replied, matching his tone. Then, seriously, "If we are observed, we want them to think you are carrying on an affair you don't want your parents to know about."

"I really have wanted to see you," Lee said.

"Sorry the old woman put you through such a hard time," Cheetah commiserated. "Who'd have thought she could yell at you for almost three hours at her age!" She shook her head. "And she looks as though she's about to keel over."

"How did you know what happened?" Lee asked, surprised.

"We have other contacts in your home," Cheetah told him. "You didn't think we were going to turn you loose in that bank without someone to watch you, did you?"

Lee shook his head in amazement. Cheetah leaned over and put her hand on his arm. "I am really sorry it was so rough," she told him again.

"It was nothing," he said flippantly. "Just words."

"I know better than that, Lee. I only hope she didn't shake your commitment to our cause."

"No chance," he stated flatly, wondering just how convincing he sounded. He drove on for a few minutes in silence.

"Find a nice place to park," she said at last. Lee was glad to oblige. It was a beautiful day and a beautiful section of the country. He pulled over at an edge of a curve overlooking a wide valley, green with new rice. Cheetah snuggled next to him and pulled his arm around her.

"We want anyone who may be watching to think you like me," she said impishly, "so you'll just have to pretend."

"There's no need to pretend. You know I—" he began, but was cut off sharply by the businesslike tone of her voice.

"Now let's get serious. How are things going at the bank?"

"Father has used me in several departments this week," Lee answered, not mentioning the janitorial work. "But it looks as though he is going to end up with me in the loan department."

"Can you help us from there?" she demanded. "Do you handle the money?"

"Not really," he admitted. "I just work on the loan applications."

"Can you get into the safe?" she insisted.

"No."

"Then you'll have to get yourself moved," she ordered. "We're not interested in just having you there. You've got to get yourself placed in a key spot."

"But I'd have to be there for years before I have access to large quantities of cash," he protested helplessly.

She seemed to be thinking about that. While she was silent he began to play with a tuft of her hair by her right ear. She seemed to be snuggling closer to him than the job would require. Turning his head, he kissed her on the left side of her forehead. She placed her hand on his chest as if to push him away, but she didn't push very hard.

"You're distracting me," she said, more by way of imparting information than delivering a rebuke.

"Just trying to make our cover look good," he lied, not even trying to sound convincing.

She smiled up at him. He interpreted it as an invitation and kissed her. She responded warmly and he kissed her again. She laid her head against his chest for a few moments, then sighed and pulled away.

"That's enough. We've made our point," she remarked succinctly, seemingly ignorant of his intentions.

"But—Cheetah—" he pleaded.

She wouldn't listen. "No!" she demanded, the old snap in her voice once again. "No more. It's too hard. Drive us back."

"What do you mean, it's too hard—?" he began, but she cut him off again with determination.

"Drive!" she fairly screamed. Confused, he started the car and headed back toward town.

"About the bank," she said in a businesslike tone after a few minutes of silence, "you must be looking for every opportunity. It is extremely important. By the time we meet again, I want you to be prepared to give me a plan."

"I'll try," he promised half-heartedly, still disappointed.

"We will not meet for two weeks. That should give you all the time you need."

"Two weeks!" he protested indignantly.

She smiled impishly, once again in control of the situation. "Is that not enough time—or too much?"

"Too much," he stammered, sounding foolish even to himself. "It's not enough time to plan the robbery, but it's much too long not to see—" Again he was cut off abruptly by her sharp retort.

"Don't start that! Ever! You know better. If a few minutes of relaxation is going to make you lose all control, how do you suppose we are ever going to execute this project?" She paused, then continued in a lower tone of voice, "But you do wonders for a girl's ego."

"Don't tease me," he said sullenly.

"I'm not teasing. Not about the job, anyway. I will contact you in two weeks. Be ready." They drove in silence for a while, then she said suddenly, "Let me out at the next corner."

As she stepped from the car she reached across the seat and touched his cheek, whispering, "See you soon." Then she hurried away.

For the next two weeks Lee was confused and frantic. He wasn't sure how much of Cheetah's behavior was a part of the cover and how much was real. His desperation was heightened by his need to find a way to help Toto rob the bank. The better he knew the bank, the more impossible it seemed. There were all kinds of safeguards built into the system and he knew there was no way in which he could familiarize himself with all of them.

Finally he abandoned the idea of being able to get into the huge vault and began to consider other possibilities. A daytime holdup while the vault was open seemed suicidal. In addition to the bank being in the center of the commercial district where traffic made fast escape impossible, the guards had been trained to slam the vault shut at the first hint of trouble. The bank was so large it would take an army to gain control of the whole place and stop anyone from sending an alarm to the police headquarters. And if they couldn't get into the vault, a daytime robbery would be ridiculously risky for the comparatively small amount of cash that could be taken from the tellers' drawers.

Lee started thinking about the tellers' cash drawers. Each teller started out the day with $6,000 in his drawer, this amount having been balanced and prepared the evening before. There were eleven such drawers, making a total of $66,000. It was nothing compared to the millions in the vault, but at least it was attainable. Lee began to concentrate his thinking in that area.

Late the next afternoon a messenger brought a letter to Lee in the bank. He was surprised to find that it was from Cheetah and it sounded like a love letter. As he began reading the sentimental message he quickly realized that it contained a coded directive. Applying the simple letter substitution code they used, he realized she wanted to meet him the next night. The letter specified the time and the place.

In the Lee home, the evening meal, served promptly at eight, was a ritual presided over by his grandmother. Lee's grandmother not only approved the menu, she also determined the topics of conversation.

Again and again in the weeks since Lee's return, his grandmother had directed the conversation into a discussion of the advantages of the capitalistic free-enterprise system. Assuming that she believed his story about having worked as a merchant seaman during his recent absence from the family, Lee could not help but wonder why the old woman kept belaboring the point. It made him uneasy. Perhaps his father had told her of Lee's earlier radical leanings, Lee speculated, and his grandmother was merely trying to reassure herself that he had undergone a change in his thinking.

Nevertheless, Lee rather enjoyed the discussions and participated as though he were the most ardent capitalist in the world. He could see that his father alternated between admiration and incredulity at Lee's procapitalist contributions. Each time, Lee would think he had his grandmother convinced that he agreed with her, only to have her bring up the topic again a few days later.

This night she wanted to talk about the international monetary implications of continued encroachment in industrialized countries. Lee had responded with avid interest for the first hour, but as the time for his scheduled meeting with Sylvia approached he became nervous and frustrated. Eventually he stopped participating, hoping the conversation would drag and his grandmother would tire of the discussion. But it turned out to be another one of those evenings in which the old woman seem perfectly satisfied to listen to herself.

Just after ten o'clock Lee's mother politely excused herself. Lee took advantage of the break in the conversation to suggest to his father that he thought he would like to take his dog for a walk. This idea apparently pleased the grandmother, who had always deplored Lee's apparent lack of interest in the pedigreed wolfhound his parents had given him years before. She encouraged him to go, and, as he left, Lee heard her telling his father that this added evidence of a sense of responsibility in Lee was a good sign that he was settling down to business.

Lee hurried Chow past all the spots the dog wanted to sniff until they finally arrived at the corner of the park where he was supposed to meet Sylvia. Shortly thereafter she appeared. As soon as she saw Lee she rushed up to him and gave him the customary kiss, then took him by the hand and pulled him toward a park bench away from the light.

"We will continue to use the 'illicit romance' front," she whispered in an intimate tone. "I think you like it, anyway." She laughed gaily, continuing the pretense for the benefit of anyone who might chance to overhear them.

"You are very observant," Lee replied with mild sarcasm. "Why is it that you are a day early?"

"An emergency arose that I need to tell you about," she said. "Are you ready with a plan?"

"I have an idea," he said vaguely. "But first—what is the emergency?"

"Toto suspected that one of the men who survived the trap Susong fell into might be a police spy. That would explain why the police didn't pursue them."

"I don't get it," Lee replied. "Why would the police miss the chance of tightening the noose on Toto? If they had a man in the camp, they would have known we couldn't stop them."

"Toto suspects they want to know the whereabouts of the weapons stockpile," she explained. "They may be waiting until their informer knows where it is."

"What can Toto do?" Lee inquired.

"He's already done it. He set a trap to see if the spy would expose himself. It worked. So Toto let the other survivor of the ambush execute the spy."

"Why did he do that?" Lee growled. He still did not like this business of summary executions.

"First, because the other man had been made a suspect and had been endangered by the spy. Second, if the other man happened to be a policeman, too, he wouldn't want to shoot his buddy."

Lee nodded, but he didn't like it. "If it is all over," he demanded, "then what is the emergency?"

"Toto was afraid the spy may have fingered you before we got rid of him," she said. "You are to be extra careful and very alert."

"As usual," Lee said with a confidence he did not feel.

"Tell me your idea about the project," she said, changing the subject.

"Tell Toto there is no way to get the big prize, but he could pick up sixty-six big ones without much risk." He paused to let that sink in, then added, "I just hope he's not greedy."

She shook her head thoughtfully. "He's not going to like that. It's hardly worth coming in for."

"Well, it would be fine with me if we just called it off," Lee shrugged.

"It's not likely," she replied. "Whatever the reward, it will be worth it to throw them off balance. I'll see what Toto thinks and be in touch with you as soon as possible."

Lee nodded absently.

"Now kiss me," she ordered. As his face drew close to hers she whispered, "Just part of the cover, you know."

He kissed her. And the way she responded didn't strike Lee as being just an act.

4 Bank Robbery— Failure and Flight

Lee remained nervous and tense throughout the following week. He had a feeling Toto was not going to be satisfied with a mere $66,000.

It was now Lee's custom to walk the dog in the same area every evening. There were several places where Cheetah could make contact with him if she so desired.

Eight days after his last contact with her, he stopped one night on a dark corner and struck a match, a prearranged signal that all was clear at that spot. Suddenly Toto's voice came softly from the building behind where he stood.

"Move over here and lean against the wall," he hissed.

Lee was surprised as well as disappointed at hearing Toto's voice. He'd looked forward to seeing Cheetah. Without seeming to acknowledge Toto's presence, he obeyed the instruction.

"I am disappointed with the bad news you gave Cheetah on the prospects for our project," Toto said sternly. "Are you convinced that it is the best we can do?"

"I am convinced that attempting anything more than that would literally be suicide," Lee said firmly. "We must either strike during the night or have an open fight with the police. And it is impossible to open the vault at night."

"Why is it impossible?" Toto asked.

"Because there is a timing mechanism. It takes two keys plus the proper combination to open it at any time. And once it is shut in the evening, it cannot be opened until the next morning." Lee paused, then added as an afterthought, "And if it is not properly closed by a prearranged time, it triggers the police alarm."

Toto did not speak for several minutes. "That sounds pretty bad," he agreed at last. "What is your plan?"

Lee continued to appear to be leaning casually against the wall. In the darkness he could not even see Toto, but could only hear his voice.

"The only possibility I see is to try to switch cash-drawer inserts. The cash drawers have metal trays which are like cash boxes. These are taken to the vault after they have been checked and filled for the next day. I think I could substitute empty trays for the full ones between the time they are taken in and when the vault is closed."

"Then would it actually be necessary for us to enter the bank at all?" Toto asked.

"Yes. We'd still have to enter because I couldn't get the money out. We would have to take the key from my father. I think I could get us by the security guards without having them trigger the alarm. I've gone back to work a few evenings just to get them used to seeing me there after hours. I would have to overpower them after I get in, then let you in to get the money. What do you think?"

"Can't you get any other money out of the vault?" Toto inquired.

Lee thought for a while. "Maybe I can. I'm not sure. Let us say I will have the $66,000 set out, and anything else I can get."

"Well—" Toto hesitated. "If that's the best we can do—it's better than nothing."

Lee breathed a sigh of relief. "Good. It needs to start at my home on an evening my father is there. You'll force your way in, take his key, and pretend to take me hostage. Let him think you're going to try to blow the vault. He'll be so sure you can't do that, he won't even be concerned. We'll be long gone before he realizes what actually has happened."

"It's not exactly what I had hoped for," Toto was still complaining. "But if that's the best we can do—"

"I'm sure it is. We could even trip the alarm intentionally as we are leaving. It will take the police about ten minutes to get there, so we'll be gone." Lee chuckled suddenly. "We can even leave some propaganda leaflets behind. Let them know who did it. It will really upset people to know we were so bold!"

"Yes," Toto said, now enthusiastic. "I like that. The army is still up north and we are down here. That will really shake them up." He paused, then went on. "It won't take your family long to realize you were in on the plot, though. I'd hoped to leave you on the inside for future use."

"It can't be helped," Lee answered him. "My father and my grandmother are already suspicious, anyway. They would never trust me again. They are not even sure about me right now."

"Fine," Toto said absently. "You'd better go back now."

Lee stalled. "Is—Cheetah around?" he asked. "I need to make arrangements with her for our next meeting."

"She is watching in the back," Toto said. "No need for you to see her. When you are ready for us, just send word to your cook that you would like to take a lunch to work with you that day. We will strike the same evening."

Lee was amazed. "The cook!" he exclaimed, realization slowly dawning. "Lu Ching has worked for our family for years! How—?"

"Never mind," Toto said, cutting him off. "We will wait for your word. Not less than three days, nor more than ten. Good luck."

Lee turned and began walking back toward his house. Things were finally coming to a showdown. He'd be glad when it was over.

For the next few days everything went perfectly. Lee located eleven unused cash-drawer trays and stored them in an empty cabinet in his office. Then he began making frequent trips into the vault. He wanted the people to get used to seeing him there, and he also wanted to see where other large quantities of cash were kept.

The days were slipping by. A week had passed since his talk with Toto. Then came another lucky break. He'd been trying to figure out what evening his father would be home when his mother inadvertently answered that question for him.

"Do you have anything planned this evening, Kiki?" she asked that morning at breakfast, using her pet name for her son.

"Nothing special. I thought I might do a little extra work at the office," he said gratuitously.

"And you, Solomon? Will you be home this evening?" she inquired of Lee's father.

"I suppose so," he told her. "Why do you ask?"

"I thought it would be nice to have a quiet family evening together. This is mother's day to play Mah-Jongg. She will be tired and will retire early."

"All right," Lee's father agreed.

Lee turned to the maid who was removing the breakfast dishes. "Please ask the cook to make a lunch for me to take to work today," he said casually.

His father looked astonished. "You're going to take a lunch?" he asked in apparent surprise.

"I'm tired of the restaurants," Lee said. "And if I'm not going to work this evening, I should get some extra work done during my lunch hour."

"Good thinking," his father agreed, evidently pleased. "You have been showing a serious side lately—one I'd begun to fear didn't exist in your playboy nature."

"Now, now, Solomon," Lee's mother cautioned. "Lee hasn't been a playboy since he came back from his—his journey. If you recall, he hasn't even been dating anyone."

Lee bowed his head in embarrassment. He wasn't in the habit of discussing his social life with his parents. He felt uncomfortable and wished the conversation would end.

"I've noticed," his father said. Then, to Lee, "And since you have made it clear you are not going to allow us to choose a wife for you, I think you had better get busy and find one of your own." He arose, indicating that the conversation was finished.

Lee's day at the bank was filled with tension. He was able to transfer a large quantity of old currency to his office, worn-out bills which ordinarily would be separated by the tellers and returned to the government bank. Lee had no idea how much he had or what portion of it they would be able to use, but it was a start. On two occasions he was nearly caught in the vault by other employees. By the end of the day, he was so jumpy he could hardly control himself.

The substitution of the cash-drawer trays had been carefully planned and had gone without a hitch. By the time he arrived home for dinner that evening he'd begun to relax a little. He'd even started looking forward with anticipation to the action planned for the evening.

As the family finished their leisurely meal without the grandmother present to dominate the conversation, Lee's mother announced, "My brother Samuel plans to drop by shortly."

Lee was taken aback. He certainly didn't want anyone else to be here when Toto arrived. His father, however, was the first to protest.

"Your brother! I thought you said you wanted a quiet family evening!"

"Wang is family," she said defensively.

"Uncle Wang is a religious nut!" Lee exploded. "And I'm in no mood to see him."

"Kiki!" his mother reproached him. "You and Wang used to be such great friends. Wang is very disappointed that you haven't visited him since you returned."

Lee felt uncomfortable. It was true they'd always been good friends until his uncle had gone to work with some kind of religious group up north and Lee had got involved with the radical element at school. Then everything changed. The one time they'd seen each other since then, they'd argued violently. Lee didn't want to see Wang. Wang seemed to know Lee better than Lee knew himself, and he was afraid Wang would see through the act he was putting on. He'd probably see through the "kidnapping," too.

"He just wants to see you, Kiki," his mother was saying.

"In that event," his father said, "I may as well leave."

"No! You can't!" Lee blurted without thinking. His father looked at him in surprise. "I mean—" he explained, "you can't leave me here to talk with that fanatic alone!"

Lee's father seemed pleased at the thought of his son identifying with him rather than with Wang. "Very well," he agreed. "We'll face him together."

Lee was relieved, but annoyed. Complicity with his father was not really what he'd had in mind, but it would serve to keep his father from leaving the house. That was the important thing.

A short time later the maid entered the room quietly and announced Samuel Wang. Wang came into the room behind her. He was a little more gray than Lee remembered, but still straight and impressive.

"Good evening, my sister. Good evening, brother-in-law," he said, bowing courteously. Then, warmly, to Lee, grasping his arms in both his hands, "And good evening to you, my dear nephew."

In a short time, despite Lee's reticence, he and Wang were talking and thoroughly enjoying their conversation—so much so that Lee nearly forgot about the plan for the evening. He was relieved that Wang didn't jump right into a discussion of religion. He seemed more interested in recalling pleasant times they had shared. Since Wang was just ten years older than Lee and had lived in their house before going off to college, the two of them had shared many enjoyable experiences.

They were laughing together over one particular incident, when they were suddenly distracted by a commotion at the front of the house. A moment later, a group of armed men silently filed into the room and quickly took their positions along the walls.

Lee's mother stifled a scream. His father attempted to assert his authority and gain control of the situation. "I demand to know what you are doing," he spluttered indignantly. "How did you get in here?"

Lee looked from one of them to the other until at last he caught Cheetah's eye. She was disguised as a man. She gave him no sign of recognition or response.

Toto spoke at last, between clenched teeth. "Your servants are tied up in the courtyard. We are a contingent of the People's Liberation Army and we are going to liberate some of the people's money from your bank."

"Impossible!" Solomon sneered.

"It had better not be," one of the men threatened menacingly, waving his gun at Lee's father.

"You will come with us and open the bank and the safe," Toto told him.

Solomon shook his head. "The vault cannot be opened at night. It has an automatic timer," he replied with complete confidence.

"We are not interested in your excuses," Toto snapped. "Just come with us." An armed man stepped forward and grabbed Solomon's elbow, shoving him roughly.

"No!" Lee cried, jumping toward his father.

"Leave him alone!" Lee's mother pleaded as Solomon suddenly began to clutch his chest. His knees began to shake and he slumped into the nearest chair. "He has a bad heart. You will kill him!"

"Leave him alone! You don't need him!" Lee shouted. "I'll take you to the bank myself."

Toto eyed him coldly. "Can you open the safe?" he demanded.

"I can take his keys and do as much as he can."

Toto hesitated. "But I want him, too," he insisted.

Lee could not understand Toto's determination in the matter. Maybe he was just trying to make it look convincing. "It won't do you any good to carry along a dying man!" Lee argued. "Leave him here. You don't need him."

Again Toto hesitated. Then his eyes fell on Wang. "Who are you?"

"I am Samuel Wang."

"He is my uncle," Lee volunteered.

"Oh—you're related? Good. We will take you instead," Toto said.

"No!" Lee cried, suddenly feeling genuine concern for Wang. "I will be your hostage. You don't—"

Toto cut off his protest in a loud voice. "Shut up! You're not in charge here. I am." Turning to one of his armed men, he said, "Take that one out and tie him up in my jeep." He indicated Wang with a jab of his forefinger.

Lee's mind was whirling. What in the world was going on? Why did they take Wang? He did not understand.

"Get the keys," Toto ordered. Cheetah obeyed.

Lee's father had slumped to the floor. He was breathing heavily and had turned an ashen gray. Lee's mother was on her knees beside him, weeping helplessly.

"We're taking this one, too." Toto said to Lee's mother. "Do not call the police or they're dead." She stared, terrified, as one of the armed men pushed Lee out of the room. All the way down the hall and out the door Lee tried to stop and talk to Toto, but the man kept pushing him ahead. When they finally got outside, Lee turned on Toto.

"What is going on?" he demanded angrily.

Toto ignored his question and went on barking orders to the

men. Suddenly an old peasant woman emerged out of the darkness and came rushing up to Toto.

"Mister Captain! Mister Captain!" she repeated, trying to get Toto's attention.

"What's the trouble?" Toto asked, turning to face her. Just then Lee recognized her. She was Lo Wan, the old woman from the hills, disguised as a beggar.

"The police! The army! They are there." She tried to whisper, but panic gave her shrill voice a sharp edge.

"Where?" Cheetah cut in.

"At the bank. They are hiding in the alleys and the side streets all around the bank!" She was gasping so, she could barely finish the sentence.

Toto began to mutter softly under his breath. Cheetah blurted, "We've been betrayed!"

"But who—?" Lee gasped.

Toto eyed him coldly. "You?"

"No!" Lee snapped. "I—I'm giving everything I've got—"

Cheetah cut him off. "It was not Lee," she said, defending him. "It was that police spy!"

"But you said he was dead," Lee reminded her.

"The other one. He must be a spy, too. That's why he got himself assigned to one of the watch positions, so he would be out of danger when they slaughtered us!" Cheetah spat out her words angrily.

"You must be right," Toto agreed. "We've got to try to get out of here. They probably are setting up roadblocks—but maybe they're not ready yet. It's our only hope."

"What about our men on the other side?" Cheetah asked. "We've got to warn them."

"Lee," Toto ordered, "you take Cheetah in your car. She will show you where the others are. Warn them, then scatter. Make it quick. Surprise is our only chance."

Lee ran toward the garage with Cheetah right behind him. As he jumped into the sports car he heard Toto's jeep pull away. He hoped that they had left Wang behind. The engine roared to life and he pulled out into the street.

"Go left to the boulevard," Cheetah ordered. He followed her orders, his mind racing over the events of the evening.

"Why did he try to take my father?" Lee asked Cheetah. "And why did he take my uncle?"

"Since we weren't getting much from the bank, it seemed advisable to kidnap someone for ransom. Turn left at the next corner," she continued calmly.

"But that was not part of the deal. I could have told you my father has a bad heart. Why wasn't I consulted before—?"

"Oh, shut up!" she snapped, interrupting him rudely. "Who do you think you are? You're not running the operation. You're just one little soldier. The commander is not going to consult with you." Her voice was heavy with sarcasm and ridicule. Then, in the next sentence, her tone changed as though she were then talking to a different person. "Turn right at the next corner. Go slowly. They should be right up ahead."

Lee drove slowly with the lights off. Ahead he could see the outline of a jeep. "There they are," he said. "Shall I pull up alongside?"

Suddenly Cheetah screamed. "That's not them—it's the police! Step on it!"

She grabbed the wheel and pulled the car into a hard right and down a side street, then Lee pushed the accelerator to the floor. Just as they swerved into the side street the jeep opened fire on them. They quickly took another sharp corner before the gunmen could get the range.

"Head out of town on the boulevard," Cheetah said.

As they picked up speed, Lee was thankful to know he was driving one of the fastest cars around and he knew how to handle it.

"How did you know that was the police?" he asked her.

"I saw their taillights," she pointed out. "And I knew we had covered ours."

As they sped along, his mind darted back to their earlier conversation. "Whose idea was it to kidnap my father?" he demanded accusingly. "Yours?"

After a long silence Cheetah answered quietly but firmly. "I'm sorry, Lee. I knew it would hurt you, but you have got to rise above your personal wishes. It was the best thing we could think of under the circumstances. And it was for the cause."

"The cause!" he spat out the words bitterly. "If my father is dead, it will be your fault."

"I am sorry," she stated flatly.

In the high-powered sports car, Lee had quickly deserted the jeep that had fired at them. It looked like it would be no problem getting away. They were already through the suburbs when Cheetah cautioned him, "Be careful. They frequently set roadblocks on the other side of this rise."

He let up on the gas, but it was still nearly too late when they crested the hill and saw that the police had pulled two heavy farm trucks across the road. Seeing he couldn't stop in time, he pulled the car to the right, slammed on the brakes long enough to start a skid in the dust of the shoulder, then cut a hard left. The low-slung sports car fishtailed, then skidded into a 180 degree turn. With cool presence of mind, Cheetah fired her submachine gun into the midst of the parked trucks, blowing out their tires and starting one on fire.

Lee jerked the gearshift into low and roared back in the direction from which they'd just come. They were back over the crest before the police could recover enough to begin shooting at them.

"What now?" Lee asked grimly.

"Are there any side roads off the highway along here?" she asked.

"There's a rough dirt road that goes through to that road we parked on a few weeks ago." Even as Lee spoke, he was reminded of the incongruity of this experience as compared to the other one.

"Take it," she ordered. As they turned into the rough country lane, they saw the headlights of the pursuing jeep approaching.

"This could get rough," Lee admitted. "He can go a lot faster on a road of this type than I can. This car is so low, I'll just tear the bottom out."

She did not reply, but kept a close watch out the back. The headlights got closer and closer. Soon the jeep was close enough to open fire on them although the shots were wild.

"Can you stop us without your taillights coming on?" she asked abruptly.

Lee replied, "Of course."

"Then do it—as soon as we go over the top of this next hill."

When they were over the rise, Lee expertly geared down and had almost stopped completely when the jeep cleared the hill less than fifty meters behind them. Cheetah fired directly into the engine of the jeep and then screamed, "Go!" Lee accelerated as rapidly as the rough terrain permitted, leaving the stalled jeep in a cloud of dust.

"Well done!" he shouted over the noise of the moving car as it bounced roughly over the road.

"Thank you, sir!" she quipped, sounding smug.

In a short time they had come to the country lane Lee had spoken of. Turning, he picked up speed. "We may have lost them," he said hopefully.

"I doubt it. They probably have this road patrolled, too. Keep a sharp lookout ahead. If you see anything coming, I want you to drop me off, then pretend you lost control on the next curve and crash the car. Be careful not to get hurt."

Lee glanced at her, contemplating a sarcastic reply to her last statement. But before he could think of what to say, he saw headlights up ahead.

"There they are!" he cried out.

Alert, she tensed, her catlike eyes narrowing shrewdly. "They've seen you, too. Drop me in a low place where they can't see you stop. Make the accident look good."

He skidded to a stop. Cheetah jumped out and he pulled quickly away. The next curve provided the kind of spot he needed—a curve on a rise with a sharp drop off the shoulder.

He floored the accelerator and shot wildly across the shoulder and down into the ravine. He had always enjoyed the challenge of difficult and unusual driving experiences, but this time he thought he was losing control as the rocks tore at the bottom of the car and threatened to jerk the steering wheel from his grip. The vehicle finally stopped against a steep embankment, leaning almost completely on its left side.

He sat still for a few moments as the dust settled. Taking a quick inventory, he decided he was not hurt. Headlights probed the darkness over his head and he realized the police jeep was stopping where he had gone off the road.

He'd have to play this very carefully, now—to keep from getting shot while he surrendered. And the longer he could stall, the more of a head start Cheetah would have. As he unbuckled his seat belt and began to push his way to the right side of the car to get out, he began thinking about what kind of story he could make up to tell the police. He wondered, too, if his father had died.

He peered cautiously out the window to see if the police were going to shoot first or give him a chance to surrender. Up on the edge of the road he saw three figures clearly outlined in the glare of the headlights.

"Stupid idiots!" Lee thought aloud. "If I wanted to shoot, they'd be perfect targets."

The words were barely out when the clatter of machine-gun fire filled the night air. *Cheetah!* his mind shrieked. She was firing on them! At that moment the figures seemed to jump into grotesque positions, then they tumbled down the slope into the ravine.

Lee's mouth went dry and he shuddered. Somehow it hadn't bothered him before. It had been like a game, to shoot at some faraway figure and to be shot at. But now, watching those three men blown to pieces at close range, and without warning—Lee stood rooted numbly to the ground, his stomach turning over. Then Cheetah's voice called to him.

"Are you hurt?"

"No," he managed weakly, not wanting to talk to her.

"Then hurry up. We've a long way to go before sunrise."

He managed to scramble back up the slope, carefully avoiding the mangled corpses. He felt weak and sick by the time he reached the top. She watched him stagger the last few steps and asked, "Can you drive?"

"I'm still shaken up," he admitted.

"Very well," Cheetah volunteered calmly, "I'll drive. I know where we need to go, anyway."

They climbed into the police jeep, Cheetah leading the way. She drove, taking the first dirt cutoff that headed toward the hills. Lee slumped back, trying to block the scene of those falling bodies out of his mind—but the only other thing he could think of was his father lying still and gray on the floor. He felt hot anger rise inside him against the vicious female in the jeep next to him until at last he was riding along with his fists clenched.

They drove for several hours along the back roads without headlights, yet Cheetah never missed a turn. She was calm, efficient, controlled. Lee was filled with revulsion. *She has the grace of a cat,* he thought with disgust, *the eyes of a cat—and the morals of a cat!*

As the first light of dawn became visible in the east, Cheetah drove into a heavy tangle of underbrush. "Help me cover this jeep so it can't be seen from the air," she ordered.

Lee pulled some vines across the back of the vehicle. Cheetah took off her male attire, revealing a peasant blouse and shorts underneath. She used the discarded uniform to carefully wipe off the machine gun and then threw the clothing into the jeep.

"Let's go," she said, motioning to him. She started into the jungle at that same rapid pace he remembered. As they walked she removed her headband, letting her short hair down. The transformation was complete. She was no longer the rebel soldier. She appeared instead to be an innocent schoolgirl.

"Are you all right?" she asked at one point when she stopped for breath.

Lee merely nodded. He didn't want to talk to her. They walked on. The sun was up and Lee decided it must be around eight in the morning.

They walked into a clearing and Lee recognized the hut where he had stayed when he was wounded. He didn't think it was very smart to come here. After all, the police spy would know about this place. He followed her into the hut, trying to tell her that.

"Lie down here," she ordered, giving him a look of forced patience and taking a length of rope from the shelf behind her.

Comprehending, he obeyed. She began to tie him securely. He was on his side, facing the wall. She finished binding him, then he heard her walk across the hut and sit down. He was too angry, too frustrated and tired to try to figure out what she was going to do now. He dropped off into a troubled sleep.

5 Trial and Imprisonment

"This is the police. Throw out your weapons and come out with your hands up!" The amplified voice boomed through the little thatched hut. Startled, Lee tried to jump up before realizing he was still tied up. "You have thirty seconds," the voice continued, "and then we will open fire!"

"Don't shoot! Don't shoot!" Cheetah's voice implored, screaming. "They are gone and we are tied up. Please don't shoot."

Astonished, Lee twisted himself around to look at her. He hadn't realized she was still in the hut. Wild and disheveled looking, she lay tied up in the far corner, weeping. A helmeted head peered cautiously around the edge of the door, surveying the situation, and then the soldier stepped into the hut.

"All clear," he yelled, propping his gun against the wall, With a glance at Lee, he went over to Cheetah and tried to comfort her as he began to untie her. Other soldiers and policemen poured into the hut and one of them began to cut Lee's ropes.

"You must be the hostage they took," he said, and Lee nodded. "Who is the young lady?" he went on. "We didn't know they'd taken a female prisoner."

Cheetah stood inside the protective curve of the soldier's arm, looking like a helpless schoolgirl. Before Lee could answer, her rescuer spoke. "Captain, those red devils have been holding this little girl for more than a year!" Cheetah leaned against him for support and acted helpless.

"How long ago did they leave?" the captain inquired of Lee.

Lee stammered uncertainly and Cheetah answered. "They dropped him off a little after dawn, and then they left."

"How many were there?" he asked.

"Only two. Unless some stayed outside."

The captain frowned. "No. There are only two left. We have the rest of them."

Cheetah seemed to brighten. "Did you catch that horrible Commander Toto?" she asked eagerly.

"Yes," the captain said. "Toto was injured when his jeep tried to crash through a roadblock, but he will live to face trial."

"I am glad," she replied. "He is the one that—" She covered her face as if ashamed to continue.

The soldier patted her shoulder comfortingly. "Don't worry about him!" he said. "He is going to pay for it."

Lee suddenly thought of Uncle Wang. "Did Toto have another hostage with him?" he asked the captain.

"Yes. He had two of his men and a hostage in his jeep when he crashed. His men were killed and the hostage was injured."

"He is my uncle!" Lee said desperately. "Is he badly hurt?"

"I'm afraid so," the captain told him. "The wreck caught fire before they could get him out."

Lee groaned, clutching his head in his hands. If only Uncle Wang hadn't come to see him. If only Cheetah hadn't decided to kidnap someone. As his concern for his Uncle Wang mounted, so did his contempt for Cheetah's cold-bloodedness and her phony act.

"Come on," the captain said to the soldier holding Cheetah.

"You get these two back to town, and we'll see if we can pick up the trail of the other two."

The soldier took them to a clearing about a half mile away, where the vehicles were parked. As they rode into town with the soldier, Lee was appalled to hear Cheetah fabricate a long tale of her captivity at the hands of Toto. The soldier believed every word.

They were taken directly to the headquarters camp of the national police where they were given a royal welcome. Cheetah, particularly, was the center of attention, the police even permitting the newspaper people to interview her. She repeated the account of her alleged captivity, sounding very convincing.

During the commotion, however, a plainclothesman came over to Lee and, taking him by the elbow, led him from the room, down a corridor, and into another room. Facing Lee squarely, he spoke.

"Lee Kai-chang," he stated formally, "we have been informed that you were not actually a hostage of the rebels. You were, in fact, a member of their rebel band and were aiding them in their attempt to rob your family's bank. I am therefore placing you under arrest."

Thus began the seemingly endless ordeal which was to change the course of Lee's life. For the next seven weeks, until the government brought him to trial, he was kept in solitary confinement and was permitted to see no one except his lawyer, through whom his family notified him that his father had recovered from the heart attack and that Uncle Wang, too, would live, although the effect of his injuries remained uncertain. Wang had suffered fractures of the back and the right leg and had been severely burned.

Lee's attorney had found out that a police spy had infiltrated Toto's group and was going to reveal the whole operation in court. Toto, although badly injured in the crash, would stand trial. Lee was sure that Cheetah's testimony would destroy Toto and he found himself wondering what it would do to him,

now that the truth was known about his rebel activities. His
contempt for Cheetah by now had turned to white-hot anger
and he wondered how he had ever been attracted to her to
begin with. He was not permitted to have a newspaper, radio,
or television while in solitary confinement, so he hadn't
realized what a big thing the government was making of the
trial until it began. As court convened and Lee entered he was
astonished to find that the courtroom was packed and that
news photographers and television cameras were everywhere.

It was obvious that the government was exploiting the entire
affair from a standpoint of sensationalism. The government
witnesses described detailed plots and atrocities having nothing to do with Toto's group, but no one objected. The purpose
of the trial was evidently to make a spectacle of the offenders
for the benefit of the general public more than to find out the
truth and to administer justice.

The police spy turned out to be the one who had been with
Commander Susong. He spent days reiterating the details of
his experience with Susong's band and, after its defeat, with
Toto's rebels. He made his own participation sound very
heroic, including his murder of the other Susong man, who
was also a police agent. He pointed Lee out as the one Toto
had told his band was their "man on the inside." His testimony
alone was enough to convict Lee, and Lee began to wonder if
he would be executed. It was obvious that the prosecution
intended to ask the court for the death penalty for Toto.

And then the prosecution called as their next witness Sylvia
Chung. Lee snapped to attention as Cheetah entered the
courtroom, dressed in demure schoolgirl attire and looking
scrubbed and innocent. Lee was appalled, wondering how she
could perpetuate this charade. Surely the spy had implicated
her, too.

In a soft voice Cheetah described the abuse she had
experienced—and witnessed—at the hands of Toto's men
while being held captive. She told how Toto had forced the
noble police spy to kill his companion. When asked by the

prosecution how she was treated while in captivity, she shyly confessed to having been molested and abused again and again, making Toto's group look like a bunch of sadistic fiends. She did, however, single Lee out as being different, saying he'd always treated her well. She left the impression that Lee was a rather naive playboy who didn't really understand Toto and his objectives and who was being used by them. Lee's lawyer caught this part of her testimony and began at once to build his defense accordingly.

The trial went very quickly after Cheetah's performance. Both Lee and Toto were found guilty, and Toto was sentenced to death. Lee was sharply reprimanded by the judge for being so foolish and for allowing himself to be used by the communists. His sentence, under the circumstances, was light. He was given one to three years in prison. He could thank Cheetah that it was no more than that, but he wondered why she had protected him and what she'd be up to next.

His mother visited him. She cried a lot and it made him feel uncomfortable, especially when she said she was praying he'd find God. He was glad when she left. He was happy, however, to learn that Wang was improving after a series of operations and skin grafts, although it was not certain that he would walk again.

Cheetah visited him, under the guise of Sylvia Chung, pretending to be a casual acquaintance. She said she hoped he would find friends in prison, and her tone and manner indicated that there would be certain people in prison that he'd be expected to cultivate. She promised to visit him regularly and he felt, somehow, that it was more a threat than a promise. As Cheetah, she aroused his anger and contempt, but, as Sylvia she evoked a certain fearful distrust. It was a puzzlement.

Lee had always been vaguely aware that the prison system in his country was bad, but there was no way in which he could have been prepared for conditions in the national prison to which he was taken. It consisted of six large "barns" enclosed in a high, gray stone wall. Each barn held several hundred inmates, all of whom were locked in one large bull pen. The guards made no effort to enter the buildings for any reason. They simply patrolled the open space between the buildings and the wall.

Lee was stripped and given a pair of black cotton shorts, and was then marched barefoot into the compound. Four heavily armed guards in turn escorted him to the steel door of one of the buildings, ordered the inmates back from the door, pushed Lee inside, and locked the door behind him.

He stood in the dark shadows and surveyed the area. The large, heavily barred windows in three walls were crammed with men hanging onto the bars, trying to get a breath of air. Along the back wall, three six-foot-wide shelves ran from side to side, serving as beds. Below the bottom shelf he saw movement which he suddenly recognized with horror as a pack of rats. Besides the men hanging on the bars, there were two other groups in the room. One group of effeminate-looking men sat brushing one another's hair and picking lice from their heads. The second group was made up of weak, sick-looking men slumped or lying on the bottom shelf just above the rat pack.

Lee moved slowly around the room. It was a far cry from the luxury he'd always enjoyed at home. He hadn't known such filth and human degradation existed anywhere. He was certain that his face betrayed the revulsion he felt, but it didn't matter. Everyone ignored him. As he was making his second circuit of the bull pen, a man stepped toward him from the window and spoke softly.

"Greetings, Comrade Lee. Welcome to the Imperialist Palace," he said sardonically.

"I assume you are the friend Cheetah told me about," Lee answered under his breath.

"Cheetah?" the man said. "I don't know that name. Nevertheless, we are your friends. You must join a gang to survive here, and you must be invited to join. I am inviting you to join my gang. We are number three."

"Number three? What does that mean?" Lee inquired.

"At mealtime they push the rice trays through those slots in the wall," the man explained. "Group one eat all they want and then feed their 'pets' over there—" he indicated with a nod of his head the group of effeminate-looking men. "Then they let group two eat. When group two have had all they want and have fed their 'pets,' then we eat. Then group four, then five, and whatever is left the 'singles' over there eat. They don't get much," he added.

"How do the groups get numbered?" Lee asked.

"We fight for it. The Killers are in control here. They are by far the strongest. Last year the Balat gang challenged them for number one, but two of their men were killed and two others had their eyes gouged out. Last week the Balats' leader finished his twenty years and left. We are about ready to challenge them for number two. Can you fight?"

"I have a karate black belt," Lee said. "But why bother? What difference does it make whether you eat second or third?"

"Group two gets meat or fish sometimes," he was told. "We never do. That's worth fighting for." He paused, then added, "I'm not sure your black belt is going to help you much in the kind of no-holds-barred fighting we will do."

"Well, I've also had hand-to-hand combat field training in Commander Toto's camp," Lee said defensively.

"Good. The two together may make you useful. We'll need all the help we can get. The Balats are still tough. And another thing is sleeping space. Number one and number two take the top bunks on hot nights and the second bunk when the weather is bad. We have to take what they leave."

"What about the bottom bunk?" Lee asked.

"The singles fight it out down there with the rats," he replied. "Come on over and meet the gang. They're not all comrades. We don't talk much about those things here. We just try to survive. This is our window. If we knock off the Balats, we'll move to that one. It's better because it gets more shade. We take turns on watch all the time. The Tokolates would love to move up to number three, so we have to watch them. Either group would rather catch us by surprise than let us pick the time. We must always be alert."

As he spoke, they moved over to the window. The introductions were very elementary. The other inmate simply stated, "This is our man. He will be on fourth guard team."

No one said anything. The circle opened slightly and let Lee move in. Lee had the strange feeling that he was not a man, but a fighting animal, being accepted into the pack.

The days flew by in a tension-filled struggle for survival, turning into weeks. Lee existed from day to day, concentrating his efforts on doing just that, forgetting about the outside world and trying to keep his mind off his home and family. He could not bear the contrast.

Then Cheetah paid him a visit. The guards came to the door and called for him. When he went out, they escorted him to a small, barred window in the wall. The four guards stood behind him as he faced the window. Cheetah stood outside. She was disguised as Sylvia, but she was still Cheetah, Lee thought. As much as he hated her, it was still a relief from the boredom and monotony of prison life just to see another face.

"Hello, darling," she said.

Lee blinked in disbelief. Every time he came in contact with her, she surprised him. "Hello," he said. "Thank you for coming."

"Did our friends welcome you?" she asked solicitously.

"Yes, and I'm fine," he told her. "But I've got to talk to you. How could you hand Toto over to them like that?"

She smiled lightly over his shoulder at the guards, but her eyes were cold. Slipping into Chinese, she spoke. "He knew he was a dead man as soon as he was captured. He would not have allowed them to take him alive if it weren't for the accident. He understood. We planned it long ago."

"When will he be—" Lee began, also speaking in Chinese.

Her face turned hard. "He was shot by a firing squad at a public execution last week."

Lee felt a chill go through his body. "But how did you get away with it? The spy knew you," he reminded her.

He had to have some answers. He didn't care about the guards, although Cheetah seemed very much aware of their presence. They looked dumb and uninterested, but she was cautious. She lowered her voice and looked past him at their faces as she replied. Lee had to lean forward and read her lips to catch her answer.

"The government liked the reaction my story was receiving from the public. They were more interested in its impact than they were in the real truth. Besides, the spy didn't want to make me look very important. It would have made him look ridiculous to have been ordered around by a girl."

She smiled lightly, changing the subject. "But let's talk about happy things," she said archly, a mocking tone in her voice. "I have become great friends with your grandmother." She was no longer using Chinese.

"You—what?" Lee stammered, not sure he heard her right.

"Your mother thinks I saved your neck," she said sweetly. "She looked me up after the trial and gave me a place to stay at your house. Your grandmother and I like each other very much."

Lee was stunned. He'd heard right. "You're living in my house?" he asked, already knowing.

She affected another artificial smile. "Isn't it wonderful? I just love your family. They've been so kind. I've even met your Uncle Wang, in the hospital. He's doing very well. The skin grafts are taking and they're optimistic about his back."

Lee was relieved to hear Wang was improving, but very upset to know that Cheetah had moved in on his family under the guise of Sylvia Chung, particularly after causing them so much trouble. He wondered how long she planned to stay— what her plans were. Knowing Cheetah, she'd be up to no good. Her very tone and manner, in fact, told him she had something in mind.

"I can't believe you're living in my home," he said at last. "What are you—doing?"

"Nothing, really," she smiled, taunting him. "Your mother feels I should just take it easy, after my ordeal in the jungle."

Lee was filled with helpless rage. "But why?" he demanded. "What are you after? How could you just—?"

"I've got to live somewhere, don't I?" she asked innocently.

"Oh, come on!" he said impatiently. "What are you up to?"

She gave him a long, hard look and a nasty smile. "I want to become friends with your family," she replied casually, adding with a shrug, "after all, it will be so much easier after we are married."

Lee felt sudden panic. "Married?" he gasped. So that was it!

She smiled and winked, obviously enjoying his speechlessness. "Don't worry. I haven't told a soul yet. But I can hardly wait." She turned away, blowing him a kiss. "I'd better go now. I'll be back as soon as they'll let me." Then she disappeared.

Lee returned to the building in a daze of shock and anger. Once the prospect of marrying Cheetah would have been exciting, but now he was sickened at the thought of bringing such a creature into his family. *As bad as this place is,* he thought, *I'd rather stay here in prison.* Still, he knew Cheetah. And if Cheetah had made up her mind to marry him, she would do just that. Filled with helpless frustration and rage and feeling the need to strike out at someone, Lee suddenly attacked the nearest Balat man and the long-awaited fight was on!

Cheetah visited Lee three times in the next three months, telling him that the officials permitted only one visit per month. Although he was lonely and longed for a break in the monotony, he was thankful she could come no more often. Under the guise of her silly, gushing schoolgirl chatter, she made it clear that she considered herself his commanding officer and expected him to follow the strategy she had worked out. This fact only intensified the frustrated rage that possessed him when he thought about her living in his home and deceiving his family while plotting a way in which to destroy them. He hated her, and he was consumed with the fear and dread of being forced, eventually, to marry her. At last he could think of nothing else.

Cheetah had reported that Wang was improving rapidly and was even talking about the possibility of visiting Lee. Consequently, Lee was not surprised, but only pleased, when the guards came one day and told him he had a visitor in a wheelchair.

6 "And the Truth Shall Make You Free"

As Lee approached the window to see Wang he was determined not to reveal surprise. Cheetah had warned him that the accident had changed Wang—that he looked much older. In spite of the warning, however, Lee was not prepared for what he saw. Instead of the tall, strong, dignified man he remembered, Wang was now a bent, shrunken figure in a wheelchair. Lee steeled himself against letting his voice or his manner betray what he felt.

"Hello, uncle," he said, smiling. "So good of you to come."

Wang looked up. "Please forgive me, dear friend, for being of no value to you in these hard months!" Lee was relieved to note that despite his obvious handicaps, Wang's eyes were still sharp and there was a ring of self-assurance in his voice.

"Of no value!" Lee replied. "You were the one who needed help. And I could not help you. In fact, I was at fault—"

"Not so!" Wang interrupted. "You must not think that. I was at your home because the Lord led me. You were in no way the cause of the accident."

"But I am guilty, Uncle Wang," Lee argued. "I was the one—"

"No!" Wang insisted, raising both hands. "Above all the circumstances of life is my sovereign God! Nothing can happen to me that He does not permit."

Lee pondered his last remark for a long moment. He looked at Wang, old before his time, deep physical suffering etched in his face, and shook his head slowly. "If your God allowed all this to happen to you when He could have prevented it, then He is not a good God," Lee said despairingly. "He is a hateful devil."

Wang did not appear shocked by this blasphemy. He seemed, in fact, to find it easier to accept than Lee's feelings of guilt.

"My God is a God of love," he said calmly and confidently. "He has the highest good for all His children continually before His eyes. He constantly intervenes in the affairs of men to turn their acts of sin and rebellion to His purposes."

Lee was torn between astonishment and contempt. "If you can show me how the senseless pain you have suffered—" He didn't bother to complete the thought. It was too ridiculous. Instead, he jumped to his own situation. "If you can show me one single iota of decency or good in this prison—or in Cheetah—" Her name slipped out before he realized it.

"Who is Cheetah?" Wang asked, puzzled.

"Never mind," Lee cut him off. "She's not important. Your continued faith is more ridiculous now than ever before."

Wang gave him a look of compassion. "I don't mean to add to your problems, my friend. Let's talk of something else. You look haggard. Are you quite sure you are eating enough?"

Lee smiled grimly. "We are number two now. That means I get all I want to eat—even fish and meat on occasion."

"Can I bring you anything?" Wang inquired.

"I would like some fruit," Lee admitted. "But if you bring it, you will have to bring enough for these men, too." He indicated the guards with a toss of his head.

Wang smiled at the guards. "I will gladly do so," he said. "I will come next week."

Lee shook his head. "They won't let you come next week. You can come only once a month. Besides, it's too hard for you to come in—in your—" he faltered, not wanting to mention the wheelchair.

"Nonsense!" Wang said. "I can come every day if I want to. And the wheelchair is no problem. It's quite portable."

"But Cheetah said—" Lee began, then stopped as realization came.

"I would like to meet this Cheetah. A girl, I presume? She seems to be much on your mind," Wang ventured. Lee nodded. Wang continued, "Sylvia would be hurt to know that there is another girl visiting you. You realize that she has fallen in love with you."

Lee stood speechless, waiting for Wang to continue.

"Sylvia says it hurts her so to see you here. Yet she faithfully comes out here two or three times a week, sacrificing every cent she can scrape together to bring you things you need." There was a note of rebuke in Wang's voice.

Lee felt sudden anger rise in his chest. "Every two or three days! Is that what she tells you? It is a lie!" His voice became loud and harsh. "And she has never brought anything!"

Wang watched him, surprised, speechless, his eyes questioning. Lee knew he could trust Wang. In desperation, he made a quick decision. "Listen, Wang," he whispered, lowering his voice, "you and I have always been friends. I need your help. I—I will never marry Cheetah!" he blurted vehemently, not realizing the incongruity of what he was saying.

Wang was totally confused. Puzzled, he asked, "Who is Cheetah?"

Lee exhaled audibly, suddenly aware that he'd lost Wang, and exasperated with himself and the whole situation. "Sylvia," he said simply, "is Cheetah!"

"I do not understand," Wang said, looking perplexed.

"Sylvia is a fake. She was never a captive. She was vice-commander of the rebel band. She is a hard-line, dedicated communist and a cold-blooded killer!" Lee could see that his

words had caught Wang completely by surprise. He looked
stunned. Lee went on. "And you may as well know the whole
story, Wang. I am a communist, too."

Wang shook his head resolutely. "I do not believe that."

"Well, at least I have been trained as a communist," Lee
explained. "I was a full-fledged member of the rebel gang. I
was not being used, as it appeared in court. I helped plan the
whole thing."

Wang didn't seem surprised. "I suspected that much," he
confessed, "although I do not understand why. And I don't
believe you really accept the communist philosophy."

"Perhaps not," Lee admitted. "But it doesn't matter
whether I do or not. I am a communist. Cheetah is my commander, and she has ordered me to marry her when I get out
of prison!"

"Hmmm," Wang mused thoughtfully. "That is serious." He
was silent for a moment, pausing with his chin in his hand.
Then, looking up, he continued, "But I disagree that whether
or not you accept communist philosophy is unimportant.
Philosophy is just another word for your whole attitude toward
life. When you say this girl is a liar, you reveal that you believe
there is such a thing as truth. All your present conflicts revolve
around the fact that you know in your heart that there are
things that are true, holy, and right. Your communist training
demands that you reject these concepts. Hence, the conflict.
Can you honestly reject all standards of righteousness and
simply give obedience to anything your communist superiors
tell you is right?"

Lee shook his head slowly. "Once I did. But no longer."

Wang continued. "Then you must accept the fact that there
is a God who has established objective standards of righteousness. When we conform to those standards, we are right.
When we do not, we are wrong."

Lee listened attentively.

"This wrong is what the Bible calls *sin*," Wang explained.
"Rebellion. Disobedience. You can dress it up and call it *intel-*

lectual doubt, but that doesn't change what it is. God calls it sin. And God says the wages of sin is death."

Lee looked around him at the hopelessness and degradation of the prison surroundings. *No doubt about that,* he thought.

"But listen to this," Wang went on. "God didn't just set the standards. He also provided a way of escape from the hell we make for ourselves when we violate His standards. No matter who we are, no matter where we are, or what we've done, He can set us free!"

One of the guards prodded Lee from behind with his gun, evidently in contempt of the conversation he'd partially overheard.

"I want to talk further with you about this, uncle," Lee said earnestly, "but my companions are getting restless."

Wang directed his attention to the guard and asked, "May I give him this book?" The guard stepped forward and took the Bible from Wang, leafed through it to see that there was nothing inside, then nonchalantly handed it to Lee.

"That is the Word of God," Wang said. "Just read the first three or four chapters of John's Gospel. We will talk tomorrow."

"I will," Lee replied. "But I should warn you that I'm not a candidate for conversion. A communist is too far from God ever to find Him. Everyone knows that."

Wang smiled confidently. "You don't have to find God, my nephew. He has already found you. On the other matter," he added as the impatient guards began to push Lee back toward the building, "don't be concerned. We can handle that, too—with God's help."

Wang came three times in the next five days, always bringing something to eat and something to read. The prison gang complained that all Lee ever did was read. For a while they ridiculed him then finally left him alone, for which he was thankful.

He read through the entire Gospel of John and on into Acts.

He found it necessary to read and reread. His mind rejected so much of what he read—yet, he remembered what Wang had said about intellectual doubt. Wang had said *unbelief* is *disobedience.*

He and Wang didn't talk much about Cheetah. She somehow did not seem such a big problem anymore. When she would come to his mind, he'd simply close her out, think about something else. He'd decided he was not going to marry her and things would work out. He was more interested, for the time being, in resolving his inner conflicts and finding out the truth.

Truth. Such a simple word. Yet, a word laden with such deep, profound meaning. He found it frequently in his Bible. Realizing this, he began marking the passages where it was found, and he was thus impelled to read on, to discover everything this book had to say about truth. It was an intellectual exercise, a quest for knowledge, and a way to divert his mind from the horror that surrounded him. Nothing more.

And then one day he read, as if for the first time, John 8:32: "And ye shall know the truth, and the truth shall make you free." Lee pondered this. How he longed to be free! But surely there was some deeper meaning here. He read on, in John 8:36: "If the Son therefore shall make you free, ye shall be free indeed." *Free? Behind prison walls?* Lee wondered. *What a supreme contradiction!* He decided he'd concentrate his efforts on the passages that spoke of truth. Being free, under the circumstances, was rather unlikely.

In John 14:6 he read where Jesus said, "I am the way, the truth, and the life . . . ." There it was again—that word *truth.* As he read on, these words seemed to leap off the page at him again and again. He'd have to discuss this with Wang. He read on and on until at last the slanting rays of the setting sun cast the shadow of iron bars across the pages of his Bible and he could no longer see.

But he could not sleep. The Scripture passages kept running through his mind in startling succession. Deep inside him there was a strange longing, a persistent yearning, and he decided at last that maybe he should try to pray. This was all new to him. And there was no way that he could get out of the bunk and kneel without creating a commotion. Anyway, he didn't want to be down there with the rats. He wondered if God would hear him anyway, if he didn't kneel, and decided to give it a try. He turned over on his face and cradled his head in his arms.

"Jesus," he said, under his breath, "I do not know You. But if You are who this Book says You are, I want to know You. If You can and will show me how, I'd like to give You a chance with my life. Uncle Wang seems to know You very well. Can You help me?"

Lee would never be able to find the words to explain to anyone what happened to him in that moment. It was as though a light went on inside him, radiating all around him. It filled him, warmed him, permeated his very being. All the doubt and fear and cynicism in him suddenly began to break up and melt, like an ice float in the river in springtime. The ice was melting. The river was rushing, rushing, overflowing its banks, flooding his soul.

Nobody paid any attention to him. The sound of men weeping at night inside prison walls is not at all uncommon. Even the hard, tough ones cry sometimes. And no one cares.

Wang had never pushed Lee to become a Christian. He'd only answered his questions, tried to help him understand difficult parts of Scripture, and shown love and concern. Sometimes he'd help by giving him a few questions to find the answers to in the Bible, as an assignment. Yet, he did not seem to be at all surprised at his next visit to see Lee's excitement and his obvious joy as he clutched the window bars with both hands, oblivious to the guards standing nearby, and exclaimed, "I've got it, uncle. I've got it! I've met Christ, and He's real to me now. These prison walls can't hold me any longer. I'm free!"

Wang's face lit up and his eyes clouded over as he registered joy and relief, but not surprise. "Praise God, my friend," he said quietly. "Praise God—brother!"

One day when the guards said he had a visitor, he went eagerly to the window in anticipation of an exciting conversation with his uncle. He was visibly disappointed to see that it was not Wang, but Cheetah, who had come.

"What's the matter, dear? You seem unhappy," she said. Lee merely shrugged, resenting her solicitous tone.

"I'm sure this terrible place is getting you down," she sympathized. "But it should be a good learning experience, too. It will make a real proletarian out of you. You've had it too soft all your life."

He was irritated by her superior tone and by the knowledge that she was enjoying all the comforts of his home while talking to him about having had it too soft. "To treat a man like an animal can accomplish nothing but to make an animal out of him," he snapped.

Cheetah raised her eyebrows in surprise. "Many of us have been treated as animals by your class all our lives!" she retorted.

Lee remained calm. "At least," he told her, "any treatment you may have received was never a part of a planned program to make an animal of you. I think that your concept of equality is to pull everyone down to the animal level."

She studied him with narrowed eyes. "I can see that you are going to have to be reeducated," she said menacingly.

Lee was not intimidated by her. "I am being reeducated now," he said significantly. "I've never before had such a hunger for understanding in all my life. I spend all my time reading."

"Reading?" she asked. "Reading what?"

"I am reading the Bible."

She registered shock and surprise. "The Bible? You know better."

"I've changed my mind," he announced confidently. "I have become a Christian." It felt good to say it aloud to someone, *particularly to Cheetah,* he thought.

Her eyes flashed angrily. "You have fallen under the influence of your uncle," she accused. "I was afraid of that!"

"Wang has been helping me," Lee admitted. "But you are the one who motivated me to seek the truth, so I must thank you." He watched as she shook her head slowly and he enjoyed seeing her self-confidence shaken. "You made me question how the better world I was seeking could be won by vicious, hateful murders," he said, his boldness increasing by the minute.

Cheetah was enraged. "Wang will pay for this!" she spluttered. "And you—you will have to be eliminated!" No longer did she sound like a love-stricken schoolgirl. *Her true colors are showing again,* Lee thought. *And they are red, red, red. Red is the color of my true love's philosophy.* He laughed aloud, and this only seemed to infuriate her even more.

"You'd better be careful, Cheetah," he said, sobering. "Wang knows all about you. We decided that he would write up the whole matter and file the report in his safety-deposit box. If anything should happen to us, it will be sent to the police and you and your whole operation will be exposed."

"You can't prove a thing about me," she bluffed. "And you don't know a thing about our reorganized movement."

"You don't know what Toto shared with me before the trial," he reminded her. "Remember, he expected us to work together." He could see that she was upset by that. She knew Toto had thought highly of Lee, and she had no way of knowing that they hadn't seen each other after they were arrested. Lee continued, "And you can't imagine what all your friends here in prison have told me."

"What do they know?" she bluffed, sounding uncertain.

"Never mind," Lee said. "Let's just get something straight. You are to move out of my house, break all connections with my family, and leave us alone—or everything I know will be reported to the police!"

"Your life would be worthless!" she snarled viciously.

Lee laughed. The irony of her remark was too much. "My old life was worthless, and it's already dead," he pointed out. "I have a new life now, and it is hidden with Christ in God. I am no longer a communist. I am a Christian. If you will do as I say, I will not expose you. I have loved you, Cheetah—and my God loves you. I do not wish to see you in prison."

"You are an idiot!" she screamed at him, her fists clenched.

"I will pray for you, that you may find the truth," he said.

Furious, she turned away. It was the last time she ever visited him. Wang reported during his visit a week later that she had disappeared. Lee's mother had been upset by the fact until Wang explained to her why Cheetah had gone. The realization that her beloved son had accepted her Lord at last was a comfort and a joy to her.

The remaining months of Lee's prison sentence went quickly. He was so involved in his devotions and the study of the Scriptures that he barely noted the passing of time. Wang and Lee prayed that the prison situation would remain stable enough that Lee could continue to study and not have to be involved in bloody fighting. Lee kept his commitment to the gang by taking his turn at guard duty. In addition, he began a literacy study for several of the men who could not read. In a short time, other prisoners showed interest in learning. As the men applied themselves to their lessons, tensions were eased and fights became rare. By the time Lee was released from prison, he had many real friends and three brothers in Christ among the prisoners.

7 The Connection

After spending a few days with his family following his release from prison, Lee went to Hong Kong as Wang had suggested and signed up for a course of study at a Chinese seminary. He enjoyed his studies, as well as the Christian fellowship, and welcomed the opportunity to share openly his love for Christ.

In Hong Kong everyone is very much aware of the ominous presence of that nearby giant, the People's Republic of China. Lee found that his various experiences made it much easier for him to talk to the communist youth in Hong Kong who tried to ridicule the Gospel. Eventually a dream began to form in his heart and mind—the dream that somehow he might be used by God inside Mainland China. He had learned that many students from Hong Kong enter the People's Republic on visits, and at last he decided to go. He wrote to Wang to see if he would like to go along.

Wang's reply indicated that he was concerned about Lee's interest in the People's Republic of China. He repeatedly encouraged him, in his letters, to forget that inaccessible area and let God use him among the millions of overseas Chinese youth who were being recruited by communist agents. This made good sense, and Lee resolved to dedicate himself to the task. But God somehow seemed to keep turning his heart and his mind to the eight hundred million or more Chinese behind the bamboo curtain.

Wang was worried that such a trip might be dangerous for Lee. But Lee had a passport in his Christian name, John Lee, and he was certain no one in the People's Republic of China would take any notice of him.

Lee had met people in Hong Kong who were praying for the Mainland, and he was aware of several research groups that tried to keep track of what was happening there. Generally, however, the consensus of Christian opinion seemed to be that there wasn't anything that could be done for China. The motto seemed to be "watch and pray" but Lee felt dissatisfied to do only that.

Then he read a book by a man by the name of Brother Andrew who had been successfully smuggling Bibles into Russia, and he knew that he had to do something. Others could do the watching and praying. He would take Bibles into China!

He shared his idea with several of the students in the seminary. They seemed sympathetic with his desire to do something, but could think of many reasons why his idea would not work in China. They told him that the borders were much more tightly guarded in China than they were in Europe, and that smuggling would be impossible. They also pointed out that there was little evidence that Christians were still worshiping in China or would use the Bibles if they could be smuggled in. And, they added, if there were still a few Christians there, they would be operating strictly in secret and he would not be able to find them.

Uncle Wang added another objection. Was this smuggling a proper activity for a Christian? Wang's letters pointed out that the Bible taught that Christians should be submissive to the government and that this mandate seemed to apply even to the communist regime in the Mainland.

But hadn't Peter and Paul continued to preach Christ even after being ordered by the authorities to stop? Did the Scriptures not say that we ought to obey God rather than man? The more Lee thought about it, the more impatient he became with all the arguments. And try as he might, he could not rid himself of the belief that God was leading him into a ministry behind the bamboo curtain. After much prayer, he decided just to step out in faith and do it.

He purchased ten Chinese Bibles from a local Christian bookstore and applied for permission to enter the Mainland. He quickly learned that the application contained many questions he wasn't prepared to answer. *Chinese name?* He hoped that their security system wouldn't be efficient enough to turn up his old record. *Reason for visiting China?* He decided his purpose would be to visit relatives. He could recall the names of several of his mother's family who were still inside and he had to admit he was curious about them. Besides, they were a perfect excuse. He listed two whom he thought were still in the Canton area.

He felt that it would be best if no one knew he was going, but he had talked so much about it at school that people kept asking him how his plans were coming along. He decided to leave suddenly, without notice. Early one morning he took the train to the border, crossed the Pearl River Bridge, and faced the border guards of the People's Republic of China for the first time.

He expected to get his suitcases and carry them into the customs area—the usual procedure at border crossings—but he was informed that his bags had been sent directly to customs and that he must wait to be called.

As he sat in the waiting room he wondered if the customs agents would go through his suitcases before he was called in. It was quickly apparent that they were calling one person at a time into the next room. It was impossible to tell, however, just how thoroughly they were going through the bags, or even whether the people were allowed to pass on into China.

Lee waited nervously. Soon, a man in civilian clothes walked by, hesitated, then sat down next to him. "You look quite nervous," the man said in a friendly voice.

"I suppose I am," Lee admitted. "I've never done this before."

The man looked at him intently. "Done what?" he inquired.

Lee tensed, suddenly realizing that this man was very likely a government agent. "I mean, going to China," he said. "It makes one a little nervous."

"It shouldn't," the man replied. "Why are you going?"

Lee was sure the man was a government agent. "To visit relatives," he said, hoping he sounded convincing. "My mother has relatives whom I have never met."

"It's a rather expensive trip to see someone you don't even know."

Lee laughed. "Just try explaining that to my mother. I tried to tell her the same thing. Apparently it distresses her very much that I do not know her sister and her niece."

The man asked several other probing questions, then moved away. A few moments later Lee saw him sit down next to another traveler. Then he became aware that there were four or five people moving about the room, questioning tourists. Some of the people were interrogated two or three times.

Lee looked at the copy of the declaration he had made. It specifically directed him to list everything he was taking in. He'd tried to get by with the notation that he was carrying a few books so that he wouldn't have to list ten Bibles. After about an hour and a half, his name was called. He went into the small room and found that his suitcases were already on the table. A uniformed agent was holding the original copy of his customs declaration. The agent stepped forward, indicating the luggage. "Open these, please," he said in a clipped tone.

Lee fumbled with the catches. After they were both opened, he looked up and realized the agent was staring at him intently. The agent pushed the first suitcase toward him.

"Empty this one," he demanded crisply.

Lee felt the perspiration break out on his forehead. "Do you mean take everything out?" he inquired.

"Everything," he was told.

Lee began to lift the clothes out, handling them carefully so that it would appear that he didn't want to wrinkle them. He moved slowly and carefully, praying that the man would tell him he could stop before he reached the layer of Bibles on the bottom. At last he had to take them out.

"Bibles?" the agent drawled with obvious satisfaction. "So you are a Christian. And you did not declare these Bibles. I will keep them."

"But they are for my relatives," Lee stammered.

"You said you are going to visit two relatives. Why would you need ten Bibles?"

Lee was speechless.

"You will have no use for Bibles in the People's Republic of China," the agent told him. "We are a people of one book, *The Thoughts of Mao Tse-tung.* You will leave these here."
[NOTE: *The Thoughts of Mao Tse-tung* is the basis of teaching in the People's Republic of China. It is available either in a condensed version or in five complete volumes.]

Lee felt sudden panic at the thought of being without his Bible. "But—can't I keep just one, for myself?" he asked.

"If you had been carrying only one, and had declared it, I would have allowed it. But—"

"I didn't know," Lee protested. "Please let me keep one. I read it every day."

The agent gave him a look of contempt and turned to walk out of the room. "I will ask my superior," he said haughtily.

Lee waited. In a few minutes the man returned. "You may keep one," he said grudgingly. "But you will be expected to bring it back out with you."

Lee hurriedly stuffed his clothes back into the bag. As he closed it, the agent said, "You may pass. Go through that door and wait for the train. Your bags will be loaded and taken to your hotel."

Lee walked to the waiting train, feeling defeated. What had gone wrong? If only he'd known how they operated. He boarded the train and sat down in an empty section. It was another half hour before the train finally left for Canton. As he waited, a depression settled over him which did not lift during the entire train trip.

In Canton the hotel had a bus waiting for those passengers who had reservations. Lee boarded with several others and rode across the city to the hotel, his gloom momentarily forgotten as he became involved with the sights and sounds of the city.

His bags were already at the hotel when he arrived. He registered and went straight to his room, impatient to spend some time in prayer and decide what to do next. Almost all of the money his mother had sent him to meet his expenses for the entire summer was already gone. Gone, too, were nine of the ten Bibles he'd purchased with some of the money. He had only one Bible left, and he didn't even know any Christians to give it to!

Falling down on his knees beside the bed, Lee began to pray. The spiritual oppression he had felt since he entered the country gradually began to lift, and his faith returned. He wasn't sure what purpose the Lord had in mind in this trip, but he was certain of one thing. The Lord had led him to China.

He took out his Bible and began looking for a likely passage to study. He began reading Nehemiah, the first chapter. Although this part of Scripture seemed totally unrelated to his situation, he felt compelled to read on. As he did so, he began to see certain parallels. In the fourth verse, Nehemiah had wept about the conditions in Israel just as Lee had wept in his spirit over the condition of the Church in China and as he hoped many overseas Chinese would weep. Glancing back to the third verse, he saw that Nehemiah had received a sad report on the remnant. He read verse two to see who had brought the report and found that it was one of Nehemiah's brethren who had been there!

Lee's heart pounded with excitement. The message was clear. Lee could at least be an observer of the conditions in Mainland China and report them to his brethren on the outside. Perhaps, then, God would raise up a Nehemiah who could do something. Again he committed his trip to the Lord, and for the first time since he had entered the country, he felt at peace.

The two weeks of Lee's visit passed quickly. He managed to locate his mother's niece and learned that her mother, his mother's sister, had passed away the previous fall. He tried to inquire of his cousin, Ling Su, about her feelings concerning conditions in China. He was dismayed to find that she had only the highest praise for the communist regime. Lee listened to her as she spoke highly of the country, the government, and the living conditions in general. He was not sure whether she really meant it. Still, there seemed to be no opportunity to share Christ with her.

Lee visited all the recommended tourist spots in China and photographed them freely, although at one place he was sharply rebuked by a policeman for taking too many pictures. He suspected that it was not really the number of pictures that enraged the policeman but the fact that he had photographed an old church which had been converted into a warehouse. The apparent lack of any evidence of religious fervor caused him much distress.

On his last day in Canton, Lee sat on a park bench across from the hotel waiting until it was time for his train to depart for Hong Kong. As he waited, he read again the passage in the book of Nehemiah that had become so meaningful to him. During his stay in Canton he had studied Nehemiah and in it had found many parallels to his own situation. As he read on, he became aware that someone had taken a seat next to him on the bench. A moment later a man's voice spoke quietly. "You are reading my favorite book."

For a split second, Lee froze. Then, slowly, he closed the Bible, laid it down on the bench between them and casually looked around. Sitting next to him was a middle-aged man.

"You know this book?" Lee inquired calmly.

"Yes. Very well," the man replied with a look of wistful longing. "It is a dear friend that has been sorely missed."

"You may have it, if you wish." Lee forced himself to speak as casually as though he were discussing the weather with a stranger. He glanced at his watch and looked at the sky. From the corner of his eye he saw the man lay his newspaper over the Bible.

"I would like to bring more of these books to those who would like to read them," Lee offered.

The man spoke evenly, but his voice betrayed excitement. "My friends would welcome them. We have waited so long."

"I am not sure how I can do it, but I will try," Lee told him. "How can I contact you?"

Lee knew the man was studying him intently. "My name is Wo Ti-liu," he said at last. "I live on Lotus Square, number twenty-seven. I would be most honored to have you visit my humble home."

The man was obviously nervous about giving his name and address. Lee repeated it several times in his mind so that he would remember it. Then he stood up, glancing at his watch. It was time for him to go to his train. The other man remained seated. "I will return as soon as possible," Lee promised.

The man nodded slightly. "It would be best if other books did not look like this one," he said, his lips barely moving.

"I'll see what I can do about that."

Lee strode away without looking back, rejoicing in his heart. He wasn't sure yet just how he was going to do it, but he knew that God had a way. Somehow, God would show him how to obtain the right Bibles and how to bring them to Wo and his friends.

The implications of that brief encounter with Wo kept running through Lee's mind. *There are Christians in China. They know one another. They want Bibles, and they are willing to take risks to get them.* Lee's step was light as he crossed the Pearl River Bridge into Hong Kong. His next job was to find Nehemiah.

Arriving back at the dormitory, Lee found a message taped to his door, evidently left there by the caretaker. The dorm was deserted for summer vacation and Lee had obtained special permission to stay there. The note instructed him to phone Samuel Wang at the Sonja Hotel on Nathan Road.

Lee threw his bags into his room and hurried out to catch a bus to Tsim Sha Tsui district. Although he was not sure what had brought his Uncle Wang to Hong Kong, he suspected Wang might have come just to check up on him. He hoped so. He looked forward to telling Wang about his trip to the Mainland.

At Wang's hotel, Lee obtained the room number, ran to the elevator and almost bumped into Wang as he exited from it just as Lee was about to board.

"Lee!" Wang burst out in obvious surprise and relief. The two embraced warmly. Then, with some embarrassment at their impulsiveness, they stepped apart and greeted each other properly.

"Good evening, uncle," Lee said.

"Good evening, my nephew," Wang replied. "I have been very worried about you."

Lee followed Wang to some lounge chairs and they both sat down, facing each other. "How long have you been here in Hong Kong?" Lee asked his uncle.

"Three days. And I have been very worried," Wang repeated, a brittle edge to his voice. "You are foolish. I don't know why I waste my concern on you."

Wang sounded really upset. Lee tried to ignore the sharpness in his uncle's voice. "What business have you here, uncle?" he inquired.

Wang gave him a long, searching look. When he spoke his voice, although still tense, seemed softer. "Your mother sent me. She asked me to try to dissuade you from your wild notions."

Lee deliberated for a moment, then decided to take the offensive. "Is it a wild notion to obey the Lord?" he asked.

Wang's features clouded. "When speaking of Satan's forces, the Lord says, 'Come out from among them, and be ye separate' " (*see* 2 Corinthians 6:17).

Lee did not relish an argument with his uncle. Still, he found himself unable to concede the point. "But, uncle," he pleaded, "Christ died for the lost. What right have we to judge that they are beyond His grace?"

"We are not judging," Wang refuted. "They have denied God and refused every godly way. They are murderers and corrupters of all that is holy." Wang's voice was growing louder and more insistent. "They are from the very pit of hell. If ever Satan was incarnate in the minds of men—"

"Wait a minute!" Lee interrupted heatedly, then suddenly realized that his tone was attracting attention. He paused, then continued in a quieter tone. "Don't forget I was one of them until the grace of God reached me. Besides, some of my closest friends have been communists. They cared for me when I should have been left to die. They showed more interest in me than my own family ever had. And many of the things they consider important are identical with biblical principles."

Wang straightened up as if to interrupt, but Lee charged ahead. "Sure. I know. They leave Christ out, and that means they're missing the key. But they are not fiends. They're people. People who really care. People who are trying with all their might to do something about the mess that the world is in."

"The communists are making it a worse mess!" Wang said defensively.

Lee ignored him and went on. "All right. So they need Christ. But so do the anti-communists!"

Wang sat quietly in deep thought, his eyes downcast, listening. Lee was still defending his position.

"I know it takes a miracle to win the heart of a communist to Christ," he said earnestly, his voice softer now. "But you and I are miracles, too. Besides, that isn't our problem. We are commanded to present Christ. The results are in His hands."

After a long moment of silent reflection Wang said, "I still think a very strong case can be made against attempting to evangelize communists."

"Perhaps," Lee answered quickly, conceding a point while closing in for the victory. "But that is beside the point. My trip was not intended for the purpose of evangelizing communists."

Wang raised his eyebrows, confused. Lee had caught him off guard, gaining an advantage in the argument. "My trip," he said, measuring each word, "was intended to help the Christians who remain in China."

"I doubt that there are many Christians in China," Wang protested weakly. "Maybe a few old people. And even if there are, they wouldn't want any contact with the outside. It would be too dangerous."

Lee waited until Wang had finished, then spoke. "Uncle, I have made contact with a secret Christian group in Canton. They want our help."

Wang looked at Lee in amazement. "That is hard to believe," he said, his voice registering surprise. "How did you do it?"

Lee told his uncle of the frustrations he'd experienced in making the trip until the Lord showed him in the Book of Nehemiah that He was going to use Lee to see the need in China and report it to others. He told Wang how, on the last day of his trip, a stranger had noticed his Bible and had spoken to him, cautiously but boldly, of their need for Bibles. Wang listened quietly.

"We've got to find some way to help them," Lee continued. "I know in my heart that there must be many other groups of Christians in the same situation. Could you stand for Christ for years and years without a Bible? Could I? There has to be a way to help them. I believe the Lord is going to lead me to a Nehemiah who will know what to do." He paused momentarily, then brightened, as though he'd just thought of something. "Maybe *you* are Nehemiah, uncle!" he added hopefully.

Wang restrained him with an uplifted hand. "Slow down, young man," he said cautiously. "I am not even sure I believe in this whole thing. You've never satisfactorily answered my objections to the unethical side of this business, you know."

"I don't have the answers, uncle," Lee admitted. "But I believe there must be answers. All I know is that I have never been as clearly led by the Lord as I was on this trip."

Wang frowned impatiently. "You know how I feel about basing theological decisions on personal experience," he retorted.

Lee was persistent. "Yes. But sometimes the Lord leads faster than I can keep up. I am sure He will show us these answers in His perfect time."

Their conversation was interrupted by the sound of someone calling to Lee from the other side of the hotel lobby. Looking up, Lee recognized one of his friends from school. The young man strode purposefully over to where Lee sat and, ignoring Wang, asked, "Well, how was your trip into the Magic Kingdom?"

Lee motioned him to silence. Wang looked puzzled.

"That's our special name for China," Lee explained to Wang. And then to his friend, "That's supposed to be a secret, Joshua. Do you want to get me into trouble?"

"But you're back now," Joshua replied. "So how can you get into trouble?"

Lee decided not to tell him he planned to go again. Changing the subject, he said, "Permit me to introduce you to my uncle, Samuel Wang. Uncle, this is a classmate of mine, Joshua Loo."

The two of them exchanged greetings and Joshua added, "Sorry I was so rude, sir, but those of us in Ruth McAllister's Bible study group have been praying for Lee. We are eager to know how the trip turned out."

"Well," Lee said hesitantly, "before such a trip could have much impact, I am sure we would have to know a lot more about conditions in China."

Joshua nodded. "That's just what Brother David said," he replied, then explained. "Do you remember that Bible smuggler in Europe?" They nodded, and he continued. "Well, that same man has a co-worker called Brother David who is working here to help the Church in China."

"Nehemiah!" Lee blurted exultantly.

"What?" Joshua asked, looking confused.

"Never mind," Lee said. "Where did you hear of him?"

"He came to Ruth's Bible study group the week after you left," Joshua explained. "He has a burden for the Church in restricted countries such as China. We spoke to him about you, and he said it was too bad he hadn't met you before you left. He knows all about government regulations and all that. I think he could have helped you."

Lee tried not to let his excitement show. "How can I get in touch with him?" he asked Joshua.

Joshua shrugged. "I don't know, but I can ask Ruth."

"Great," Lee said. "Let me know." He began to steer Wang in the direction of the front door, saying good-bye as they went.

"Where are we off to now?" Wang asked outside the door.

"To a telephone, to call Ruth McAllister. I've got to find out how to reach this Brother David. He may be the one I'm looking for!"

"Why not call from my hotel room?" Wang suggested.

"We'll use a pay phone," Lee told him. "Somebody is always listening in on hotel phones in this city." They walked down the street toward a pay phone where Lee stopped and dug some change out of his pockets. He dialed the number and waited impatiently. In a few seconds he was talking to Ruth McAllister, explaining his situation to her, asking about Brother David and how he could contact him. He listened for a moment, then paused to ask Wang his room number at the hotel. He gave the room number to Ruth, listened a few minutes more, thanked her, and said good-bye.

"She is going to call us back," he said to Wang. "I gave her your room number at the hotel. She's going to try to reach Brother David right now and find out when we can meet with him. Guess we just have to wait. Let's get back to the hotel and wait for her call."

8 New Wine

Ruth McAllister was a Canadian missionary who had worked with young people in Hong Kong for many years. Her apartment had always been a gathering place for students. In response to Lee's request, she had arranged a meeting between them and Brother David. Now, as the two of them arrived by taxi at Ruth's apartment, Lee was admittedly nervous and Wang seemed disgruntled.

"I don't see why we always have to bring westerners into everything," Wang said at last. "Can't we even talk about helping the Chinese Church without going to a westerner?"

Lee found Wang's reticence in the matter more than a little disturbing, and he felt that it was more than just the fact that Ruth and David were westerners. He could not understand what was bothering his uncle.

"We are all a part of the body of Christ, uncle," he admonished Wang. "That's what you have always taught me. Wouldn't it be silly of my eyes to refuse to use my tongue to tell what they see, just because they are a different color?"

"Don't preach nonsense sermons to me," Wang snapped. "You know what I mean."

Ruth met them at the door, greeting them in beautiful

Chinese. That seemed to please Wang somewhat, and he began to relax. Brother David had not yet arrived, so after the formalities of greetings and introductions were completed, Lee took the opportunity to question Ruth about him.

"Brother David is an American," she told him. "God is raising up men all over the world who share his vision for the suffering Church. David has been a missionary in the Orient for many years, but in the last several years God has given him an increasing concern for China. He has become very knowledgeable about China."

Wang looked uncomfortable. Just as he began to speak, the doorbell rang. Ruth excused herself, and in a few minutes she returned with a tall, stocky westerner who smiled warmly and greeted Lee and Wang in the proper Chinese manner. Conversation was spontaneous, and Lee found himself impressed by Brother David's sincere friendliness and open manner.

He was not, however, impressed by the turn of the conversation. They discussed the weather, the beauty of jade, the classic lines of the Chinese junk. *He certainly doesn't seem to be too eager to discuss my trip to China,* Lee found himself thinking. His mind began to wander and he began to question why he'd come. So engrossed was he in his own thoughts that he nearly missed David's subtle invitation.

"A friend of mine has one of the most beautiful junks in the harbor. He says I may use it any time I wish. I wonder if you might like to take a ride tomorrow afternoon. It is so peaceful out on the water."

Lee began to decline, then quickly reconsidered as David added significantly, "It's a great place to talk."

"Of course," Lee smiled. "I think that might be a great way to spend an afternoon, don't you, uncle?"

"I don't enjoy sailing," Wang growled, although he was obviously aware of what was going on. But with some encouragement from Lee, he finally agreed to join them.

"All right," David said at last. "Meet me at Aberdeen at one o'clock. The junk is a beautiful one with colored sails. It is called *Joy of the Lord.* I'm sure you'll find it easily."

Lee rose to leave, suggesting that they share a taxi back to Central. David declined, saying he would like to stay and talk with Ruth a little longer. He suggested that they pray before parting and immediately launched into a long and fervent prayer for the Christians in China.

Lee realized that David planned to find out more about him from Ruth, later. *Good,* he thought. *If this man is risking the freedom of people on the inside, he had better be careful.* After David, then Lee, had prayed, Ruth offered a brief prayer seeking the Lord's blessing on their association.

As Lee and Wang departed, Lee waited respectfully for Wang's assessment. Wang had stayed quiet, and Lee wondered what the older man was thinking, hoping that by now he'd softened a little.

At last Wang spoke. "I have grave doubts, my friend," he said as they waited for an empty cab. After a long pause he continued. "The man has no depth. He seems too emotional to me. Never have I seen a man weep so quickly while praying."

"But," Lee said in amazement, "his heart is broken for our people! God has given him a burden!"

Wang's eyebrows lifted. "I think he enjoys playing these cloak-and-dagger games," he commented dryly.

"But he takes this business very seriously," Lee protested in defense of David as they got into the cab. They rode several moments in silence, then at last Wang spoke, repeating himself.

"I have grave doubts and reservations."

"About David?" Lee asked. "Or about the whole idea?"

"I don't know," Wang answered quietly. "I really don't know."

Returning to the hotel in silence, they said good-night and Lee took a bus on out to the school. It seemed so big and empty. Lee wished Joshua or someone else were around.

Finally, he resigned himself to the inevitability of solitude and went to bed.

He spent the early part of the next morning unpacking from his trip, then took a bus to town and stopped for his uncle. It did not take him long to observe that Wang's bad mood had not lifted since the night before. Lee made a feeble attempt to cheer Wang by quoting Psalms 118:24: "This is the day which the Lord hath made; we will rejoice—" He was cut off by a sharp retort from the older man.

"Try reading that verse in its context and you will see it is talking about the day of salvation. It is not telling us to go around making light of every twenty-four-hour period."

Lee tried to control his angry reaction. "I thought a Christian could rejoice in all things," he said mildly.

Wang shrugged an apology without saying it. "You're right. I'm afraid I'm pretty unsettled about this whole thing. Well, let's get going."

They left the hotel without further comment, went to the Star Ferry by bus and were on their way across the bay before either of them spoke. Finally, Lee ventured a comment.

"What is bothering you, uncle?"

Wang took a deep breath. "Oh, I don't know," he said, sighing. "These communists—the cloak-and-dagger games— this foolish westerner—your mother—" He shrugged. Lee waited. Finally, as the ferry docked, Wang leaned toward Lee and said, "—or maybe it's none of those things." He led the way to the bus stop where they caught a crowded bus to Aberdeen.

The bay was packed with small houseboats. Thousands of people lived and died on these tiny boats without ever going ashore. As always, Lee found himself fascinated by the countless hordes. Wang, too, was amazed. He had never been here before and he could hardly believe what he saw. Forgetting his displeasure momentarily, he was busily enjoying the sights when he heard Lee calling to him.

"Over there, uncle. There's the *Joy of the Lord.* And there is David. Come on!"

The junk was anchored about forty meters out from the pier. As they reached the end of the pier they saw David waving and pointing to a small boat. The boatman, one of the crew, helped them aboard and took them out to the ship. Lee was pleased to see that Wang seemed to be having a good time and no longer appeared troubled. As they tried to stand in the small boat to climb into the junk, David laughed and waved to them from the ship.

The *Joy of the Lord,* they discovered, was certainly not a working junk although it had the same basic lines as the age-old work ship of the China Sea. It was a beautiful luxury craft, equipped with every modern convenience. Lee was enthusiastic in his appreciation, and even Wang indicated his approval and said he was glad he'd come.

"So am I," David boomed, throwing a big arm around each of them. "Praise the Lord!"

Lee looked over at Wang to see if he were offended, but Wang only smiled. They stood swaying together as the two-man crew got them under way.

Lee was eager to get down to business. But David seemed more interested in talking about the ship, the fishing, the currents, and anything else under the beautiful sun. After about two hours, they drifted slowly into a quiet bay off a small, uninhabited island. While one of the crewmen served refreshments, David became serious.

"Tell me about your visit to the inside," he said to Lee.

Lee glanced significantly at the back of the crewman who was serving them.

"He speaks very little English," David assured them. "But he is absolutely trustworthy. And he loves Jesus." Hearing the name of Jesus, the crewman turned and smiled broadly.

" 'Grace be unto you, and peace, from God our Father, and from the Lord Jesus Christ,' " Wang said to the crew in

Chinese. The crewman, smiling, responded with a resounding amen in Chinese.

"What did he say?" David asked.

"He quoted First Corinthians one, three and your man said 'Amen,' " Lee told him.

David laughed. "Sang is a really turned-on Christian," he said. "He escaped from the Mainland about ten years ago and Hudson Ting led him to Christ."

Wang was startled. "Hudson Ting? The publisher?"

"The same," David replied. "Ting owns this boat."

"He—owns it?" Wang repeated dumbly. "I didn't even know Ting was a Christian. Everyone I know thinks he's a communist."

"The anti-communist extremists say that because Ting won't let them use his paper to attack the Mainland," David explained. "They ignore all that he has done for the thousands of refugees who have escaped from the Mainland. And they don't seem to notice the clear stand he has taken for the Gospel in international conferences."

David went on to explain that there were three different ways in which the Lord seemed to be leading Christians to react to government restrictions. Some attempted to cooperate with the government as much as possible, holding back only in areas of conflict with their belief in Christ. Some cooperate with the government as little as possible and push their faith as openly as they dare. Still others maintain a totally secret faith in Christ.

"So they run the risk of losing their witness either through compromise, or through imprisonment, or through silence," Lee observed.

"That's it. So it is important for us who are on the outside not to judge our brothers in Christ for following what they believe is the Lord's leading for them," David explained, adding, "but let's not get off the subject. I want to hear about Lee's trip."

David and Wang listened quietly as Lee told them about his

trip inside China in day-by-day detail. Brother David's eyes
seemed to sparkle when Lee got to the part about Nehemiah,
but he didn't say anything. Lee concluded by emphasizing
once again the importance of doing something to help their
brothers on the Mainland.

Lee had forgotten that he hadn't yet told Wang most of the
details of his trip, and he didn't realize how moved Wang was
by his story until his uncle blurted out, "We've got to get the
Word of God to them!" Although stunned, he was pleased by
Wang's outburst and by David's booming "Amen!"

"Can you help us, David?" Wang asked.

David leaned forward. "I'm glad you asked," he said. "I
know of Lee's zeal for the Mainland, but I was afraid you were
one of the many overseas Chinese who have no interest in the
Mainland. Many people really love the Lord, but their vision
extends only to the overseas Chinese. I call them the *old wine*.
They are restricted to the traditional ways of reaching the traditional needs. Many western missionaries are old wine, too. But
we are *new wine*. God has called us to a new work in a new
way."

"Good analogy," Lee agreed. "Praise the Lord."

"But we must remember," David went on, "that the Lord
teaches that if the new wine is handled properly, both the old
and the new can be preserved."

Lee nodded slowly. He hadn't thought of that. "I'd begun to
think *you* were old wine, uncle," he confessed.

Wang pursed his lips thoughtfully, nodding. "Perhaps I
am," he admitted. "Perhaps I am. And perhaps it is why I have
been so tense lately. I've felt as though I would burst at times. I
knew that the Lord was trying to show me something, and I
guess that deep down I knew what it was. But I didn't want to
accept it. It's funny how hard you try at times to find fault when
you don't want to accept the truth. I know the Lord is in this,
and I'm willing to be a part of it, although I still feel uncomfortable about this business of breaking laws and opposing the
government."

"Perhaps I can help there," David offered. "There is a new book out which deals with that very problem. It is not in the bookstores here yet, but I have a copy. It shows us that as Christians we may have to break a few laws."

"I'm not sure I like that," Wang protested.

"It's based solidly on the Bible," David assured him.

Wang was dubious. "I can't imagine what you can do with a clear directive such as Romans thirteen."

"Look at it this way," David went on. "Do you believe the government has unlimited authority?"

"What do you mean?"

"Do you believe your government can order you to do anything it chooses? As a soldier, would you massacre innocent women and children as the Nazis did?" David pressed him.

"I don't see how I could ever do that," Wang admitted.

"Then consider the other side. Look at the fourth chapter of Acts. The apostles were ordered by the authorities not to preach in the name of Jesus and they refused to accept the order. Then they recalled from the second Psalm that they should expect the governments to take a stand against Christ. They held a prayer meeting and asked God to give them the boldness to disobey the government! Do you recall what happened then?"

Wang nodded. "God poured out His Spirit upon the whole gathering."

"Right. Doesn't it appear that God was approving their prayer and their defiance of the government order against preaching Christ?"

"That could be," Wang admitted, still deep in thought.

"I'll give you the book," David told him. "I think you will find it very thought-provoking."

Lee had been listening quietly, and now he spoke. He was eager to get the discussion back to the main point. "But what can we do for the Christians in China?" he demanded to know.

"We can get them Bibles, Scripture teaching materials, and many other things they need," David replied confidently.

Lee was astonished. "But how?" he ventured. "I couldn't."

David dismissed his remark with a wave of the hand. "With a little guidance you could have," he assured him. "That's one thing we westerners can do. We can share our experiences in Europe for your benefit. You Chinese have to be the ones to go to China, but we can help you to be more effective."

Wang still had reservations, but he was warming gradually to the whole idea. "It looks like an expensive operation to me," he said.

"It is," David agreed. "We think the Chinese church around the world should be carrying the ball financially. But until they get that vision, we are helping in that area, too."

All of Lee's questions, for the moment, had been answered and his enthusiasm for the job was beginning to stir in him a longing for action. God had given him a vision, and he ached with impatience for its fulfillment. And now God had surely sent him the Nehemiah who was necessary to make the operation a success.

"Great!" he fairly shouted. "We have the know-how and the resources. What are we waiting for?"

During the next month Lee and Wang spent as much time as possible with David. Although they were vaguely aware that he was working with others as well, he never mentioned them nor made any suggestion that Lee and Wang meet them. Each time they met they would spend a couple of hours together and then schedule the next meeting. David preferred to meet out of doors—in parks, at the beach, or on a walk up a hillside. He explained that so far as he knew he was not under surveillance by anyone, but that the work was too potentially dangerous to take chances.

Wang had moved out of the hotel and into a small apartment house quite some distance from the downtown district. Lee moved in with him to cut down expenses and to enable them to spend more time together. Wang was convinced that the only way to prepare one's self for the spiritual oppression Lee had experienced on the first trip was to be fortified with Bible study and prayer. Thus, the two of them began to spend several hours per day together in prayer, as well as in private devotions.

In addition, David had given them several books on communist theory, on the history of China since the revolution, and on other related topics. Although Lee felt that, because of his background, he didn't need to get into that kind of study, it was nevertheless a great help to Wang. Ultimately, Wang was able to pass along certain facts that brought the whole picture into even sharper focus for Lee.

They had applied for permission to enter the People's Republic of China late in the summer. If the trip was successful, Lee would be back in time for school. If not, he was prepared to finish at some other time. After much prayer, they had decided not to inform Lee's mother of their plans. Wang had tried, with the utmost care, to word a letter to her to explain his extended stay without arousing her concern or suspicion.

Late one afternoon they received a phone call, obviously from David, whose voice they recognized.

"Hello, brothers. This is your friend."

"Hello, friend," Lee replied, wondering why David had identified himself so vaguely. "How are you today?"

"As far as I can tell, everything looks fine," David said cryptically. "I think we can't be too sure, however."

Lee was suddenly impressed with the similarity of this situation to the one with Cheetah so long ago. "Under the circumstances," he ventured cautiously, "what do you recommend?"

David's reply was cloaked in ambiguity for the benefit of anyone who might be listening, but his directive was clear to Lee.

"Let us watch and pray as we hasten to the *Joy of the Lord*," he said, spacing his words as though in an invocation.

Lee understood perfectly. "Amen," he replied. "So let it be."

"God bless you and give you wisdom and discernment," David said.

Wang had been listening and he was perplexed. "What was that all about?" he asked Lee.

Lee put the phone down slowly. He knew that David was on to something. It would be best to be extremely cautious until they found out what it was.

"I would like to go out for a while," he said to Wang. "I feel somewhat stifled in here." He waved his hand around the room to indicate that someone might be listening.

Wang nodded. "Let's go, then," he replied quickly.

On their way down the street to the bus stop Lee explained, "That was David, but he didn't identify himself. He used double-talk to tell us to meet him right away at Aberdeen. He evidently thought someone was listening to the conversation."

"He thinks our phone is bugged?" Wang asked.

"I guess so. He has never acted that way before, so something must have happened. He also warned us to be very careful we are not followed." Lee glanced around casually. "Keep your eyes open and let me know if you think we are being followed, or if you see anyone you have seen before," he told Wang.

They rode the bus to the Star Ferry, bought their tickets and started the long trek down the gangway. Lee told Wang to pace himself so that they would be the last ones to board the boat. They walked at a normal speed until the crewman began to close the gate, then hurried through just as it clanged shut.

The crossing was without incident and they made no conversation. When they left the ferry landing they took a bus to Repulse Bay rather than to Aberdeen. Lee knew that both buses followed the same route for several miles. At the last stop before the two routes diverged, they got off and waited for the

Aberdeen bus. This extra precaution ensured that they had not been followed.

At Aberdeen they walked out on the pier, but the *Joy of the Lord* was nowhere in sight. They were standing at the end of the pier wondering what to do next when they suddenly recognized the crewman whom they remembered from the day of the cruise. He was paddling a small boat toward the pier where they stood.

"Misters like a good ride, huh? Very good price. You ride, huh?" he chanted, pretending not to recognize them.

Lee nodded to him and they got into the small craft. After a short trip from the end of the pier to the shore, the crewman nodded toward a parked car and spoke in Chinese.

"He will take you the rest of the way. God bless you."

They got into the car and were taken up the hillside to a small park. There, sitting under a tree and pretending to be absorbed in a book, sat David.

"Greetings, my friends. Have you come alone?" he asked cheerfully, pretending to be casual.

Wang smiled sardonically. "I hardly see how anyone could be with us after all the maneuvers we went through getting here."

David's expression became sober. "Don't kid yourself," he replied in a serious tone. "If someone really wanted to follow you, they wouldn't have been discouraged by the little bit of dodging you probably did. You might lose them if they were only casually interested."

"Can you tell us the reason why we suddenly had to go through all this?" Wang asked, impatient to know what was up.

David smiled broadly, indicating a spot on the ground with a wave of his hand. "Care to join me?" he offered. "I've brought plenty of food. Help yourselves." He produced a picnic basket from a shady spot behind the tree and opened it. Lee and Wang sat down on the blanket and began to share the food, filling their plates while David went on.

"Brothers, the life you have chosen is fraught with much pressure and uncertainty. I wanted you to get a taste of what it is going to be like."

Lee smiled, apparently undisturbed by this bit of news. But Wang seemed upset. "Do you mean to say this was just a game?" he demanded.

"Not entirely," David replied. "I have made a discovery which concerns me somewhat. This seemed to be a good way to check it out."

Lee and Wang held his gaze questioningly, saying nothing. Lowering his voice, he leaned forward and spoke rapidly.

"When I have been to your house, I have noticed a particular Chinese across the street from you who looked familiar, but I had some difficulty recalling where I had seen him before. Only this morning I saw him at the China Travel Bureau. I checked him out, and it appears that he is an agent for the People's Republic of China. Apparently his job at the travel bureau is just a front. I really doubt that he is interested in small fish such as us. I assume that it is merely coincidence that he has rented a house across the street from yours, but we needed to be sure. So I had one of our other boys follow you this morning to see if you were being tailed."

"But," Wang protested, "we watched very carefully and we were not followed."

David smiled reassuringly. "Well, our man had the advantage of knowing where you were going. And he didn't follow—he only watched to see if you were being followed. He phoned from the ferry and said it was all clear. Then our friend in the boat watched to see if anyone was behind you at the pier. Again, all was clear. So now we can relax."

"I was quite nervous," Wang admitted. "My young friend here is experienced in these matters, but it is a new adventure for me. I must admit I've felt some tension."

"There is always tension," Lee said. "I've felt it, too. It's like that all the time when you're in the Mainland, and you never get used to it."

David was quick to agree. "I've done it in Eastern Europe and it's more than just fun and games."

"Yet, it is a small price to pay," Wang reminded them. "Our brothers in there live with tension all the time."

David eyed them carefully for a long moment before he spoke. "If you two have counted the cost in every way," he said, "then as far as I am concerned, you are ready to go. When you have obtained permission, we will meet at Ruth's for prayer and then you'll be on your way."

Lee looked from Wang to David and back again, nodding in agreement. "Praise the Lord!" they said, almost in unison.

9 Reunion in Canton

Three days later, Lee and Wang had completed the necessary travel arrangements and were ready to depart. The night before they left, they met briefly with David and Ruth for prayer. It did not seem advisable for Ruth and David to accompany them to the train station, despite their mutual desire to do so, for fear of being observed. It was with a mixture of excitement and apprehension that they at last departed with the blessings of their friends.

The trip to the border was a short one. Leaving the train, they went into the government building and waited to have their travel documents examined. Afterward, they continued on to the room where the customs officials examined their bags. Because of the help David had given them, they passed customs with no difficulty. In a matter of minutes they were on the train again and headed for Canton.

"That was almost too easy," Wang said apprehensively.

Lee laughed. "Not nearly as interesting as my last trip," he observed with characteristic understatement. Although Wang appeared to be still on tenterhooks, Lee was already enjoying the challenge of the adventure. It appealed to his quest for excitement.

"I will certainly be disappointed if the people in Canton are unable or unwilling to put us in touch with another group of Christians," Wang speculated.

Lee was confident. "Relax," he said. "The Lord didn't let us get in with twenty Bibles for only one group. If they don't send us on to another group, the Lord will lead us to them in some other way."

"I'm sure you are right," Wang replied at last, sounding reassured. "It is in the Lord's hands."

Leaving the train in Canton, they went directly to the hotel. There are not many hotels in China. Only the largest cities have them and they are used almost exclusively by overseas visitors.

After checking in, they went to their rooms and changed into the drab Mao uniforms they had purchased at the China products store in Hong Kong. They had already had their hair trimmed in the style most common on the Mainland. Now, wearing the uniforms, they would be able to mix inconspicuously with the people.

Lee tucked three Bibles into his waistband and Wang did the same. They walked briskly away from the hotel and took a long, circuitous route toward the neighborhood of Wo Ti-liu, the man to whom Lee had given the Bible on his first trip to the Mainland. Occasionally one of them would stop and pretend to examine something while the other glanced back cautiously. Confident that they were not being followed, they proceeded quickly to the contact's address. Just as they turned into the doorway, a young girl ran up to them. Smiling shyly, she extended both hands in an imploring gesture.

"Greetings, my uncles," she exclaimed softly, using a Chinese term of affection. "I am Hope. We have been waiting for you. I have watched many days. Please enter."

As they entered the house, Wang whispered to Lee, "How does she know who we are?" Lee shook his head, shrugging.

"Please wait here," she said, disappearing into a back room. In a moment she reappeared, bringing with her a woman who resembled her greatly and was apparently her mother. The two of them stood side by side for a moment and Lee was astonished at how alike they were in appearance and manner. The high cheekbones—the thin lips—the delicate features framed in long, straight black hair. Suddenly the girl bowed self-consciously and ducked out of sight just as the mother began to speak.

"Please excuse my daughter," she said, smiling deferentially. "She is very excited. She is eagerly anticipating a visit from my brothers, whom she has never seen." She hesitated, as though anticipating some response, and looked directly at Lee.

After a moment of silent scrutiny, Lee said quietly to her. "We are your brothers."

The woman smiled broadly, again revealing a smile very much like the girl's. "I am so happy to hear that," she said, her eyes glowing with warmth. "Will you please be seated? My husband will be back very soon. He, too, has been impatiently waiting the return of a brother.

"Yes, I know," Lee assured her. "I am the brother he met in the park who gave him the Book."

The woman's reserve melted in the glow of her sudden enthusiasm. "Good!" she exclaimed joyfully. "I thought you must be, but I wanted to be very sure. That is the reason my daughter greeted you as she did. It would be easier to explain her enthusiasm as a childish mistake than to explain to the neighbors that we have taken strangers into our home."

"A good idea," Wang agreed.

"A good idea in the family is like a fine jewel. It is passed with care to those who will treasure it," the woman said. "It is best that we don't use our full names, but in the family I am called Happiness."

"I am Samuel," Wang replied. "And this is John."

She bowed graciously. "I am so happy to welcome you to

our humble home. Please wait while I get you some tea." She
turned and disappeared into the back room. As she left, Wang
turned to Lee.

"Let us thank God for this miracle," he said, then bowed his
head and began to pray silently. Lee, too, bowed his head in
humble gratitude for God's guidance and protection in bringing them safely to this place.

As Wang prayed, they were unaware of any movement in
the room. But when they opened their eyes there were five
children kneeling in a circle around his feet. The eldest was the
girl who had greeted them when they arrived. She was about
twelve years old, and the rest were younger.

The girl called Hope fixed Wang with an adoring look. "Tell
us a story, uncle," she begged.

"I don't know any children's stories, my child," Wang said,
looking to Lee for help. Lee only smiled. The girl went on.

"Mother said you know the Book," she urged. "They say
there are many stories in the Book, and we have heard only a
few. Please tell us a story from the Book."

As their mother quietly served tea, the older children continued to plead with them for a story while the others watched
expectantly. Wang was so moved he found it difficult to speak.
After a moment of silence, he took a deep breath and in a quiet
voice began to tell them of a boy who was reared in a carpenter's home. He described the humble home in detail. In fact,
he simply described the room in which they were sitting. The
children listened with rapt attention. Just as Wang was beginning to tell them about the boy's parents planning a trip to the
capital, there was a noise at the door and the father came in.

"Good evening, my brothers," Wo Ti-liu said. Lee jumped
up and the two of them greeted each other warmly. Then Lee
introduced Wang and the two men gripped forearms in
brotherly affection.

"I'm happy to meet you, Samuel. I am Wo Ti-liu. We are so
happy to have you in our home. I see you have met these
children of mine. I have two others. One is away at school and

the other one is in the army."

Lee was surprised to hear that. After Wo had greeted his children and they had told their father of Wang's story about the carpenter boy, Lee inquired about the other children, asking if they, too, were believers.

Wo looked sadly at his wife, then at the floor for a long moment. At last he spoke. "We are not certain. No one in our fellowship is very clear on this matter. It is one of the many things we need someone to teach us. Both our children knew Jesus when they were younger, but they found that you can progress into higher education and get good job opportunities only if you enthusiastically support the teachings of Mao thought. So first my son, then my daughter, laid Christianity aside."

Wang shook his head sadly, feeling Wo's disappointment. At last he made himself ask the question. "Did they deny Christ?"

"Not specifically," Wo replied with obvious relief. "It was not known that they were believers, so that was not necessary. But many have denied Him. Is that a sin which is unforgivable?"

Wang looked at Lee, then answered, "I do not know."

"Many of those who laid aside their faith during the cultural revolution have returned to the family," Wo told them. "Isn't it right for us to accept them back?"

"Yes," Lee said firmly. "Certainly it is right to accept them back again."

"Perhaps my son and my daughter will come back," Wo mused hopefully.

Happiness looked at her husband, her dark eyes shining. "They will come back," she said with confidence. "Did the Lord not say that He would bring our children again from the land of the enemy? We must not doubt it." She smiled, then went on, "But look. The children are eagerly waiting for their uncle to finish his story!"

Wang smiled and looked down benevolently at the children

who wriggled impatiently at his feet, hope and anticipation written on their shining faces. Leaning forward, he went on with the rest of the story of the carpenter's going to the capital, losing track of his son and returning to find the boy in the temple with the priests. "Now," he said at last, "who can tell me, who was this carpenter's son?"

The children looked at one another, smiling shyly and seeming embarrassed. Each pushed at the other and urged him to answer. Finally the eldest, the girl named Hope, spoke. "I know," she said quietly, her dark eyes radiant.

"All right. You tell us," Wang said to her.

"Jesus."

Wang placed his arm around her slender shoulders. "That's right," he told her. "Jesus, the Son of God, came to the world and lived as a carpenter's son so that we would know that He understands us." He smiled warmly at each of them, then added, "That is all of the story time for now."

"Now, you must allow us to continue our talk," Wo said to the children who in turn rose and filed obediently out of the room.

"How beautiful they are!" Wang said to the parents, and Lee nodded in agreement.

"They need much prayer,"Wo said. "It is hard for anyone to be a Christian here, and it is particularly difficult for a child. They cannot help but want to share Christ with their playmates, and their sharing brings rebuke upon them as well as suspicion upon us." He paused thoughtfully, then asked, "Do Christians on the outside pray for us? Do they know we are here?"

"Yes," Lee assured him. "Some know you are here and they do pray for you. We want to encourage more people to pray for you and for your children."

"We brought you some more Books from them," Wang declared.

Wo's face brightened. "Praise God! The one you gave me is

gone already. I am so happy to get another!"

Lee's eyes widened in disbelief. "Gone?" he said in alarm. "How could it be gone? Did they take it away?"

Wo, seeing Lee's distress, hastened to reassure him. "No, my brother. The Book is being used. I had to give it to another fellowship. But we read it much, and memorized many parts of it."

"But I gave it to you," Lee insisted. "I wanted you to keep it for yourselves."

Wo was crestfallen. "I am sorry if you did not want me to do that," he apologized. "But this other fellowship is made up of young Christians. In our fellowship, many of us have verses memorized, but in that group they need to see the Book."

Lee felt his throat tighten with emotion as he thought of these people sharing with one another the Word of God which they so jealously guarded. He knew that in other parts of the world people had free access to the Bible and rarely ever read it.

"I understand," he told Wo. "It's perfectly all right. We have more Books to give you. We will give you one for each family in your fellowship. The ones we brought are small ones with colored covers. They will not be so easy to notice."

Wo's face shone with excitement and gratitude. "Praise God!" he exclaimed. "This is beyond all that we have prayed for!"

Delicious cooking aromas had begun to fill the small apartment, and now Happiness entered from the back room where she had been busily preparing their evening meal. "We will eat our supper now," she announced, bowing slightly.

Lee was quick to protest. "Oh, we must not be a burden to you!" he declared. The idea of adding to the financial burden of this poor family was unthinkable to him.

"Certainly you will dine with us," Wo stated flatly, ushering them toward the dining area. "What would our neighbors think of us if we allowed our relatives to leave at mealtime?"

"We will be very happy to share your meal with you," Wang said. "It will be a great honor."

Happiness smiled. "The wise teacher will sit here," she said. "And the young student there." As they took their places at the table Lee smiled, pleased that Wang was taking his rightful place of leadership. Conversation was relaxed and friendly, and Lee and Wang both felt very much a part of the family.

They decided not to linger long after dinner, not wishing to arouse suspicion back at the hotel. As they were leaving, Wang asked Wo how they could contact the other fellowship Wo had mentioned earlier so that they could give the people some more Bibles.

Wo spent several moments in silent reflection before answering. Then, reluctantly, he said, "No. I think I must not tell you that. They are too vulnerable yet. If you wish to leave some extra ones with me, I will pass them on." Observing their disappointment, he added sincerely, "I am sorry."

Lee felt thwarted by this turn of events. "Our work can continue only if we are able to move from one fellowship to another," he reminded Wo.

Wo was quiet for a moment, obviously in deep thought. At last he said, "There is a brother on the other side of town. He has already suffered much, but he stands firm. I am sure he can help you."

Wang brightened. "How can we contact him?" he asked.

Wo looked from one of them to the other. "Go to the Heroes Park at noon on Friday," he told them. "Wear your western clothes. Be friendly and try to strike up conversations with people. When you introduce yourself, say, 'I am Samuel, a Christian from Hong Kong.' Most people will not understand that. But you will be able to recognize another Christian by the response in his eyes. My brother will contact you there."

"Praise the Lord!" Wang said quietly. "Shall we pray together before we leave?" They all bowed their heads, praying quietly. When they finished, Wo made them promise to return later to teach the fellowship from the Bible.

On the way back to the hotel they walked silently, in deep thought. As their pace quickened in the gathering darkness, Lee noticed that Wang had begun to limp.

"Are you all right, my uncle?" he inquired.

"I'm all right," Wang replied with some effort. "We have been very active today. First the train ride, then the long walk. These old injuries are acting up a little, that's all."·

"Oh, uncle, I had forgotten," Lee apologized. "You have recovered so well that it never occurred to me—"

"Never mind," Wang demurred. "I'll be all right after a good night's sleep."

They slept later than usual the next morning. Even after awakening they stayed quietly in their rooms for more than an hour, each of them engrossed in Bible study. Later they visited the trade fair and generally conducted themselves as tourists.

The next morning they planned to follow the same schedule and then go to visit Lee's cousin again. They had just finished their morning devotions and were putting away their Bibles when suddenly the door burst open and a uniformed man rushed in.

"What are you doing? What are you doing?" the man demanded loudly, his face turning crimson as he looked frantically around the room. Lee instinctively ducked down behind the bed which was between him and the door. Wang was the first to regain his composure and find words.

"We are just preparing to go visit a relative," he said with what he hoped sounded like confidence and authority. "What is the problem?"

"It is past ten o'clock already," the man said accusingly. "Why are you still here? Tourists go out early. They do not spend their time sitting in hotel rooms."

Lee was next to speak, rising from behind the bed. "My

uncle needs extra rest," he said, indicating Wang with an outstretched hand. "He was badly injured several years ago and he tires easily."

The man looked from one to the other, his eyes narrowed suspiciously. Then he surveyed the room carefully. After a long, hesitant pause he left without further comment.

"I guess we were acting suspiciously," Wang said.

"Wow!" Lee replied, shaking his head in amazement. "You never know what to expect. I suppose we will have to start leaving earlier. We can have our devotions in the evening. Everyone turns in fairly early in the evenings, it seems."

"A good idea," Wang agreed. "Let's get on our way now. You must take me to see our 'contented cousin.' "

They tried to behave as tourists until Friday, and on that day they scheduled their time so that they arrived well before noon at the park Wo had mentioned.

The people in the Heroes Park were very polite. They responded courteously to Wang and Lee, but no one seemed to take any special notice of the term "Christian" in their introduction. The park was becoming quite crowded with people taking their lunch break from nearby businesses, and Lee and Wang blended effortlessly into the crowd. It didn't occur to Lee that they might be under surveillance until Wang sidled up to him and said in a low voice, "Have you noticed that woman over by the wall? Don't look now, but she seems to be watching us."

When Lee was able to glance in that direction in a natural way he noticed the woman. She was wearing a large hat which partially concealed her face. Yet, it was obvious that she was looking steadily in their direction.

"She does seem interested, doesn't she?" Lee observed. "Do you think I should go over and see if I can strike up a conversation?"

"I don't think so," Wang said, shaking his head vehemently.

As they spoke, they noticed an older man standing nearby who occasionally glanced at them. When Wang introduced himself the man bowed his head slightly and returned the greeting, then stood waiting with an unmistakable air of expectancy. Wang thought he had seen a flicker of recognition to the key word, but he couldn't be certain. Wang, too, waited expectantly.

"I have brothers in Hong Kong," the man said innocuously. "But they are not satisfied there. They are seeking a better city."

Lee nodded understandingly. "We also are seeking that better city," he replied. "It is part of our reason for being here."

A look of comprehension passed among the three of them and the man suddenly seemed younger, taller as he straightened his shoulders and stood erect. When he spoke, his voice betrayed the excitement he evidently felt. "Then you must come visit my neighborhood," he said brightly. "You will see what our leaders have accomplished there."

Wang was delighted, as was Lee. "We would like that very much," he said.

The man turned to leave the park. "If you are not too busy now, just come along," he suggested to them. Nodding, they followed him, strolling casually along as they discussed the weather and other unimportant matters.

After they had gone a short distance, Lee interrupted the conversation to point out the fact that the curious lady they'd seen in the park was walking behind them in the same direction.

"Perhaps she also wishes to see our neighborhood," their friend commented indifferently. But Wang had caught a wary glance from Lee, and spoke up.

"Perhaps so," he shrugged. "But my sore leg tells me that we have walked far enough." He stopped, rubbing his thigh.

"We will try to be back in the park tomorrow if you would like to talk again," Lee told the man.

The man nodded. "Come about ten-thirty," he said, "and the park will be empty."

They parted company at the next corner as though they had

just happened to be going in the same direction. Before they had gone more than a couple of blocks, Lee noticed that Wang was limping heavily and perspiration dotted his upper lip.

"Uncle, are you in pain?" he inquired solicitously.

"It hurts a little," Wang admitted. "Do you still see the woman?"

"Occasionally I catch a glimpse of a figure out of the corner of my eye," Lee told him. "We had better just assume she is still there, and behave accordingly. We'll take a bus at the main road up ahead."

Lee was certain they were being followed by the woman, but by the time they were back at their hotel he found himself wondering if he had imagined the whole thing. They were both thrilled to have made another contact. Before retiring, they made alternate plans in case the strange woman showed up again the next day. Then, after their evening devotions, they sank gratefully into bed for a night of rest.

It was about nine o'clock the next morning when they walked to the bus stop. There were a number of people milling around waiting for the bus, about half of them women. Lee and Wang merged inconspicuously with the crowd.

"Do you see her?" Wang asked, looking straight ahead.

"I don't know," Lee said out of the corner of his mouth. "I didn't get a good look at her yesterday. She could be any of these, for all I know. We will follow Plan A, just in case. Stay alert, now."

They got on the bus and traveled to the far end of the line. As the bus began its return run, Lee spoke. "Still one on. Shift to Plan B." Wang nodded.

One stop before the park, Wang got off the bus. The woman did not get off, so Wang began a leisurely stroll toward the park, watching carefully. If all went well, he would make contact with the old man.

Lee waited until one stop beyond the park. When he got off, he noticed that the strange woman stayed on the bus. He was surprised. He, too, began a leisurely stroll back toward the park, being careful to notice the bus at its next stop two blocks down the street. Just as he'd suspected, the woman got off and started back toward him, walking at a brisk pace. He turned at the next corner and walked away from the park, evading her. But he spotted her again later and by the time he returned to the hotel that afternoon there was no doubt in his mind that he was being followed.

When he arrived at their room, Wang was already there, and Lee was somewhat concerned to see Wang stretched out on the bed.

"Do you feel all right, uncle?" he asked, entering the room.

"Fine, fine!" Wang replied, almost too heartily. "Oh, a little ache, perhaps. But what a wonderful meeting!"

"Everything went all right?"

"Oh, yes. Wonderful!" Wang sat up, speaking with enthusiasm. "We made contact again. He was so thrilled. He can put us in touch with three other fellowships!"

Lee caught Wang's excitement. "Praise the Lord!" he rejoiced. "All in Canton?"

"No," Wang said. "One in Shanghai."

"Terrific! Since we already have permission to travel there, we can make contact on this trip!"

"Let's hear about your day," Wang demanded. "I assume you feel you were being followed."

Lee nodded. "No doubt about it. The woman is very good. A professional, I suspect. Many times I lost sight of her altogether, then she'd turn up again." He sat down on the edge of the bed. "I don't know what to do now," he added lamely.

"Perhaps we should return to Hong Kong," Wang suggested reluctantly. "If the police are following us, we are only putting the Christians in additional danger."

"I suppose you are right," Lee agreed. "Although I hate to quit just when things are going so well. I suppose we must."

Wang was quiet for a moment. "Do you think we could lose her?" he asked at last.

Lee shook his head. "You know David advised against try-ing that. We might think we had lost her when, in fact, they had just assigned someone else to follow us."

"Of course," Wang suggested, "it may be just local surveil-lance. "Let's go on to Shanghai and see if we are followed there."

"We shouldn't even be talking about it here," Lee said, suddenly remembering that the room might be bugged.

"Tell you what," Wang said, lowering his voice to almost a whisper. "Let's each pray about it this evening, and before we go to bed we'll share what we have from the Lord."

"Fine," Lee agreed, adding, "I'm not sure I can get used to being the careful one trying to hold you back, rather than vice versa."

"We just want to discern the Lord's will," Wang said. Lee nodded in agreement.

And so they prayed for the Lord's will, and before sharing with the other each of them knew what the answer was. They were to go to Shanghai. They decided to leave early the next day.

The train trip to Shanghai was uneventful, except for their nervousness about the possibility of being followed. Several times they were certain they had spotted a tail, only to have the person in question get off the train before they did.

They were attempting to travel incognito. Their extra lug-gage had been left in the hotel in Canton and they were wear-ing the Mao uniforms. They had agreed to speak no English. If everything went according to plan, they would be invited to stay with their Christian contact in Shanghai.

During the last half of the trip they both began to relax and to conserve their energy for the ordeal that awaited them.

10 "And Where the Persecution Is Great, Faith Is Strong"

The address they had been given in Shanghai turned out to be a small restaurant on the outskirts of the city. By the time they arrived it was late in the evening. As they seated themselves, the proprietor, a short, stocky, balding man, approached their table and told them the restaurant was closing in a few minutes.

"That's all right," Wang said softly. "The old man of Canton suggested we stop by and try your bread."

"Do you like tea with your bread?" he inquired.

"We prefer living water," Wang said significantly.

The proprietor's eyes brightened noticeably but the tone of his voice did not change. "I'm afraid it is too late for a proper meal here," he said loudly. Then, quietly, he added, "but you must come upstairs. My wife and I will be most happy to break bread with you. Just wait for a while and I will close up."

Wang nodded comprehendingly. Then the two of them waited quietly as the man finished cleaning up and locked the front doors. When he was finished, he walked back to their table and said, smiling, "Now let us go upstairs and feast on the Bread of Life together. I just received word today that you might come. I did not expect you so soon."

"We had a change of plans," Lee explained. Almost simultaneously Wang added, "Under the circumstances it seemed advisable to leave Canton at once."

They climbed the narrow back stairs to the flat above the restaurant. It was dimly lit and very sparsely furnished.

"Let me introduce you to my wife," the man said, indicating the short, plump woman who had opened the door and now stood waiting to greet them. "You are brothers?"

"By birth I am his uncle," Wang explained. "By the New Birth we are brothers. I am Samuel and he is John."

"Then my wife is also your sister. She is called Faith. I am Cephas."

Faith stepped slightly forward and bowed, smiling. "We praise God for bringing you to our home," she said quietly. "Did you bring the Book?" Eagerness shone from her dark eyes.

"Now, now, wife. Don't rush our guests," Cephas interrupted politely. But the look of inquiry on his face betrayed the fact that he, too, was impatient to see the Book.

"It's all right, my friends," Wang said, putting their minds at ease. "Yes, we have the Book."

"Praise God!" Faith exclaimed, tears misting in her eyes and her voice cracking on the words. "We—we have not seen it in almost eight years."

"Eight years?" Lee queried. "I had thought it would have been even longer than that."

Cephas took a deep breath. "Faith carefully protected her Book for many years," he explained. "It was very precious to her—to us. But the Red guards were very thorough in their search."

"Come to the table," Faith urged. After they were seated they prayed and then began to eat their soup. Finally Lee returned to the previous conversation.

"When the Red guards found your Bible, how did you escape?"

"I was treated a little roughly," Faith admitted.

"She was beaten," Cephas corrected her.

"And you, Cephas?" Lee inquired.

Faith answered. "He was already in prison for teaching a child about Jesus."

"But is it true that they are not so strict any more?" Wang asked.

Faith and Cephas looked at each other a long time before he finally replied. "I was released from prison and Faith has not been beaten again. That is better. We have no Books. We cannot teach. It is very risky even to talk together as we are now. That has not changed."

The pain that Lee and Wang felt showed on their faces. "But if the members of the body cannot be nourished and grow and function, then the body cannot survive," Wang said desperately.

"We share our faith. Our fellowship has four secret converts and three of them are young people," Faith said defensively. "And where the persecution is great, faith is strong."

"But how can you dare witness?" Wang demanded. "In these circumstances, it would seem impossible!"

"You witness only under the direction of the Holy Spirit," she said simply.

"Then people are still arrested for witnessing," Lee asked.

Cephas nodded. "Recently a group of young men became overly zealous and spoke to some other people in the park. They were picked up and have not been heard from since."

"How long ago was that?" Wang asked.

"Ninety-one days," Faith replied quickly. Both Lee and Wang looked at her in surprise at her precise answer.

"One of the boys was our son," Cephas explained quietly.

Lee and Wang sat in stunned silence. After a moment Cephas continued. "Opposition to our home meetings has been increasing. We are afraid one of our fellowships is known to the authorities."

"What will happen?" Lee asked.

"We don't know. We are never sure. Sometimes nothing. We just have to commit it to the Lord and wait."

"We have understood that Christians have difficulty in getting jobs," Lee said. "Is that true?"

"Yes. I had no work for several years," Cephas replied. "The permit for this restaurant belongs to a distant relative. He is not well, so he is letting us operate it. If the authorities discover it, he could lose his permit."

"Is he a believer?" Lee asked.

"No," Faith replied candidly. "He just knows that Cephas is honest and that he wants work so badly that he will work for small wages."

After the meal was over, Wang gave Cephas and Faith a Bible. They spent several hours excitedly reading and discussing it until at last they were so tired they could hardly stay awake. Finally they prayed together and went to bed very late.

Cephas advised them to stay upstairs for the next couple of days. During that time they rested and read, and whenever Faith could be with them they practiced their Mandarin. Both Lee and Wang had studied it years before in school, but were still not as comfortable in it as they were in their own dialect. So they read and studied by day. After dusk, with the permission of Cephas, they took a walk in the fresh night air.

Cephas had sent word to the four other families in their fellowship that a special meeting would be held Friday evening. It was almost eight o'clock before they left the restaurant to walk to the meeting which was being held in the home of one of their members who was a government official. Lee and Wang were surprised to learn that even some government people also were Christians. Since this man lived in a private home rather than in an apartment building, meetings were a little safer there.

The rest of the group had already assembled by the time they arrived and were gathered around a radio listening to the Gospel broadcast from Manila. They were not sure why Cephas had sent word for them to gather, since he hadn't thought it wise to mention that they had visitors. And of course they knew nothing of the Bibles Lee and Wang had brought with them.

At first they were apprehensive to see that Cephas had brought strangers to their meeting. But when they learned that Lee and Wang were visitors from overseas and that they had a Bible for each family, they were overjoyed. Recovering from the initial shock, they were quick to ask Wang to teach them from their new Bibles. He complied by teaching a passage on the Second Coming of Christ and there was much rejoicing. After a time of prayer they departed, returning to their homes, deeply stirred by the experience of sharing their faith under such adverse circumstances with others who were so hungry for the Word of God.

When they awoke the next morning Lee noticed that Wang was rubbing his leg and his hip. "Is that bothering you again, uncle?" he asked solicitously.

Wang continued to apply some liniment from a jar. "Faith noticed that I was limping last night and suggested that I try this salve," he said. "It's really not too bad this morning." He continued to rub as Lee sat up and stretched, then added, "I was just about to awaken you anyway. Cephas wants to take us over to meet a brother before he has to open the restaurant."

Lee jumped out of bed. "Great!" he exclaimed. "I'll be ready in just a minute."

After breakfast and tea which Faith insisted they have, they left the apartment and hurried down a narrow lane toward town. As they went, Cephas explained to them that there was very little contact between fellowships. Christians generally agreed that it was dangerous to know others beyond their own little groups. What contact they had was usually only between the man in one group who had led someone in the other group to the Lord.

"We are very near, just around this—" Cephas suddenly stopped. As they came to the corner it was apparent to them that something was going on in the street. A small crowd had gathered. They pushed up to the back of the throng and saw several militia men shaving the heads of nine adults, both men and women. The crowd began to chant revolutionary slogans, ridiculing those being shaved as "counter-revolutionary lackeys" and "deviationists."

Cephas began to chant with the crowd and throw his fist in the air in time to the chanting. He signaled Lee and Wang to do the same. As the shaving was completed the group was herded down the street for public display. Many of the crowd followed along, joined by others who added their insults. Some of the crowd hung back and gradually turned away. Cephas turned into a convenient side street and Lee and Wang followed.

"What was that all about?" Lee asked when they were alone.

"That was the fellowship we were going to contact," Cephas said grimly. "Remember I told you that we thought the authorities knew about them? Well, that is one way they deal with the situation. Public humiliation."

"What will happen next?" Wang asked as they hurried back toward the restaurant.

"If they make public confession, they will be released."

"You mean if they just admit that they are Christians?"

"Yes, for a starter," he said. "They will be expected to criticize their antirevolutionary, antiparty conduct. They will be asked to show their sincerity by exposing others they know who are walking the same capitalist road. These self-criticism sessions can be pretty hard. You try to go along with it as far as you can. After all, there is plenty in any one of us to criticize. Sometimes that satisfies them and the storm blows over. But usually we have to refuse to cooperate at some point— perhaps at the point where they want us to expose others. That is when it gets really hard. They may send us to be reeducated, or they may send us to trial as enemies of the people."

Lee felt a tightening in his chest. "Do you think they will

expose you?" he asked fearfully.

"It is very possible," Cephas replied stoically.

As they entered the still closed restaurant Cephas turned to them and said, "It is too dangerous for you to stay here. God bless you for bringing us the Bibles. They will be treasured. Come again the next time you are in Shanghai. Perhaps we shall still be here."

At the sound of his voice Faith entered the room, a look of concern written on her usually happy countenance. "What is the trouble, Cephas?" she asked, confused.

"I will explain later," he told her. "Our friends must leave now." There was a note of urgency in his voice.

"I will get our things," Lee said, hurrying up the stairs.

"Thank you for your hospitality," Wang said warmly, smiling at them. "It has been a blessing to share your home."

Faith took both his hands in hers, her dark eyes shining. "We thank you for the rich gift you have brought us," she said. "It will continue to give us joy. Please come again soon."

Lee returned with the bags and they said a quick good-bye and left. As they walked toward the train station Wang said in a troubled voice, "I just hate to leave them like that."

"Yes," Lee agreed. "But there is nothing we can do. We can only pray that the other Christians will not be forced to expose them."

"Indeed. We ought to be praying for them right now, and for all the others, too."

"The whole body of Christ should be praying for them!" Lee declared emphatically. Then, in a voice filled with despair, he added, "Why doesn't anyone on the outside seem to care?"

"In the first place," Wang explained, "not many Christians on the outside are actually aware of the situation."

This fact seemed incomprehensible to Lee. Surely other Christians should know. Surely they would care, if they only knew.

"Then we've got to tell them!" he said forcefully.

"That's right," Wang agreed. "Assuming we get out of this mess ourselves. What are we going to do now?"

Glancing behind them again as though he suspected someone might be following them, Lee answered, "Well, we have to go back to Canton and get our bags. We'll see if our lady friend is still hanging around. If we're sure we're not being followed we can go ahead and contact those two other fellowships. We still have nine Bibles to get rid of."

"I would like to make a trip up around Peking and see if the Lord would give us a contact in that area," Wang said thoughtfully, his eyes measuring Lee as he awaited Lee's response.

Lee laughed. "You know, uncle, you are hard to get started," he announced, shaking his head, "but once you get going, it's even harder to stop you!"

Wang laughed with him in agreement, then suddenly sobered. "Christians are the only people who can laugh and cry at the same time with equal sincerity," he reflected. "I am rejoicing in the Lord for all He is doing here and also for making it possible for us to be here. But my spirit grieves for those poor brothers and sisters back there. Let us just pray silently for them while we wait for the train."

They stood in silence. Their heads were held high and their eyes were open, but they were oblivious to their surroundings. And anyone who looked closely would have seen that their eyes were bright with unshed tears.

Back in Canton they decided to conduct themselves as mere tourists for a few days in order to alleviate any suspicions that they might have inadvertently aroused. They would have enjoyed the sightseeing immensely had it not been for the fact that Wang's back and his legs seemed to be giving him more and more trouble. Lee had not realized that Wang's physical activity had been quite restricted since his accident more than two years before. His doctors had been pleasantly surprised when he had been able to get out of the wheelchair, and they were amazed when he had dispensed with the cane. However, this trip had taxed his strength beyond its limits and at last he was forced to admit that he was having difficulty in keeping up.

The third evening back in Canton they sat on a bench across from the hotel and talked. They had decided that it was not advisable to discuss their business in the hotel room anymore.

"I haven't seen anything of our lady friend since we've been back," Lee said. "Perhaps we should go and see Wo again."

"I was just thinking the same thing," Wang agreed. "Even though we had not planned to see him again on this trip, it might be a good idea since we both feel that way. But I don't feel like attempting it tonight."

Lee tried not to let his concern for Wang show in his face, but he could not help but notice that it was the first time the pain had kept Wang from doing what he wanted to do.

"Why don't you just go back to the hotel and rest up?" he said casually to Wang. "I'll walk over to Wo's place. Tomorrow we'll take a train up to Peking and see what the Lord has for us there. We need to make some effort to contact relatives up there, anyway."

"Sounds good," Wang agreed, sounding relieved. "A good night's sleep will do wonders for this old body. Give my warmest greetings to the family up there."

"Get some rest," Lee told him as he walked away. "Don't wait up for me. We can talk tomorrow."

Lee tried to be extra careful to make sure he wasn't being followed. Once he'd considered David a little paranoid about such things. *David should see him now,* he thought with amusement. Arriving at Wo's house he checked again to make sure no one was in sight, then knocked gently on the door. After a few moments the door opened just a crack, then swung wide.

"Come in, brother," Wo greeted him in enthusiastic, yet hushed tones. "This is an answer to prayer."

"Good evening, brother," Lee replied. "I was not sure whether I should come back so soon or not."

Wo ushered him into the kitchen where Happiness was

cleaning up after supper. "Generally it might not be a good idea," he told Lee as they proceeded toward the table. "But the Lord brought you here tonight." Calling to his wife, he announced, "Look who has come to see us!"

"Praise God!" Happiness exclaimed, recognizing Lee. "We were just saying that we needed to see you."

"Why? What has happened?" Lee asked.

She placed several small bowls on the table and indicated the two chairs nearest them. "Sit down for a cup of tea, and husband will tell you," she said.

They sat down and Wo began. "You've no doubt heard that there has been another earthquake in the Peking region?"

Lee nodded. "We heard the news while we were in Shanghai."

"Well," Wo continued while Happiness poured tea, "the Lord used that earthquake to reveal Himself in a very special way. In a village north of Peking a home collapsed with the eight-year-old daughter of a government official inside. When the man rushed home, he found his wife loudly praying and begging the Lord to spare her child. She had apparently been a Christian secretly for some time, and the crisis revealed the fact. It is not known whether her husband was aware of it or not. The crowd and the rescue workers paid no attention to her, assuming that her grief had driven her mad. It was obvious that no one could be alive in the house. But just before they dug down to the level where they expected to find the child's body, the mother stopped praying and informed everyone that God had told her the child was alive! Then, of course, they were certain she was mad. But when they dug a little deeper, they unearthed the little girl. She was not seriously harmed. She was not even crying.

"The crowd was deeply impressed and many of them openly acknowledged that it was a miracle. The father was so deeply moved that he made a public profession of faith in Christ, and several of the rescue workers joined him!"

"Wow!" Lee exclaimed. "Praise the Lord!"

"Amen! And the story is sweeping Peking. We thought you and your uncle would like to go up there and see if you can verify it," Happiness said.

"Wow!" Lee breathed again. "How recent is this event? And how can I contact the family? Do you know their names?"

"It happened within the past three days," Wo told him. "But you must not contact them. It would be too dangerous. You can never be too sure about new believers. Leave it to the older, more experienced Christians. They will already know how to minister to the family. You can verify the incident by talking to anyone in the area. I will give you the name of the community. If the incident has been publicized as much as I've heard, you will have no difficulty."

Lee found it almost impossible to contain his excitement. "This is fantastic!" he exclaimed. "Now I understand why the Lord sent me over here. We'd planned to go to Peking tomorrow anyway."

"You have undoubtedly heard that there have been many miracles of the Lord in China in recent years," Happiness said to him as she poured more tea.

"Oh, there have been rumors. But nothing we could really pinpoint."

"There are several others we could share with you," Wo offered enthusiastically, but Lee restrained him.

"I do want to hear about them," he said hurriedly, "but right now I must get back to the hotel. My uncle was planning to retire early. He has not been feeling well."

"I am so sorry," Happiness sympathized. "We will keep him in prayer."

Lee obtained the address of the people in Peking from Wo, then departed, promising to visit them again when he could. So excited was he about the story Wo and Happiness had told him that he completely forgot to watch to make sure he was not being followed on the way back. Arriving back at the hotel, he burst into the room, determined to share the story with Wang before he fell asleep. He was surprised to find Wang not in bed, but perched rather uncomfortably on the edge of a chair.

"Uncle, wait until you hear—" he began even before closing the door behind him, and then stopped abruptly. To his utter amazement, sitting in the room with Wang was the woman he'd seen following them before. Although her features were partially obscured by the dim light in the room, he was sure it was she. He stared at her for a moment, glanced at Wang, and then stared at her again.

"Come in, Lee," Wang said ceremoniously. "Our mysterious friend decided to pay us a visit."

"I don't think he knows me," the woman said lightly, a mocking tone in her voice.

Lee stood rooted to the spot and felt the blood rush to his face. He tried to speak, but words would not come. Then she turned and faced him, and in a hard tone he would never forget, spat out the words, "And how is my darling traitor?"

11 Wang's Collapse

"Cheetah!" As the cry escaped his lips, Lee felt his knees go so weak he could hardly stand, and the old helplessness and frustration came back like a flood. Cheetah had always seemed to be in control of every situation, and here she was again to ruin their ministry.

"Miss Chung has been sharing with me some interesting information about herself," Wang observed, evidently in control of himself. "It seems that she has lived here in China since she disappeared two years ago. Sit down, Lee, and we will let her continue."

Lee found himself astonished at Wang's calm composure. Evidently he did not consider her a threat. Or perhaps his faith that God would take care of them was greater. Cheetah was looking at him with that same superior smile he remembered so well. He managed a thin smile and sat down. "It's good to see you, Cheetah," he said politely without thinking.

"Poor Lee," she smirked. "At least you used to be a good liar. Now you've lost even that one small talent. You are not glad to see me."

"Oh, I would not say that, Miss Chung," Wang protested with all the aplomb and finesse of a formal occasion. "We are merely surprised to see you here. You know how awkward it is when you run into someone in unusual circumstances."

"Ha! That is putting it mildly!" Cheetah sneered. "You two thought you could come into the People's Republic and get away with your spying!"

"We were not spying," Lee declared. "We were only—"

Wang cut him off sharply. "We are not spies, and you know it. You have followed us all over this city, and we know that. We haven't done anything that could even remotely be considered spying."

"You certainly tried very hard to keep me from knowing just what you were doing," she snapped.

"But we didn't know it was you," Wang insisted. "It's always uncomfortable and awkward when you know you're being followed." His calmness, while making Cheetah uneasy, was helping Lee to recover his composure. "If you had merely come and asked us, we would have told you what we are doing."

"I don't believe that," she snapped. "You would have told me you were tourists."

"Perhaps," Wang conceded. "But that would have been true also. We are doing quite a bit of sightseeing, as I am sure you are aware."

"But that is not your real reason for coming to China," she insisted.

"As a matter of fact, no," Wang began, but he was suddenly interrupted by Lee.

"Uncle! She is probably working with the police!"

"No, I don't think so," Wang said confidently. "Besides, I don't mind having Miss Chung know that we are looking for Christians here."

For once Cheetah's composure was shattered. "What?" she said in amazement, her voice barely a whisper.

Wang went on in a faintly supercilious tone, his words tinged with mild sarcasm. "You know how fanatical I am, Miss Chung. I just had to see if I could find any Christians in this communist paradise." He smiled and shrugged nonchalantly.

Cheetah carefully studied their faces before responding. "How ridiculous," she said at last. "You know perfectly well that communists are atheists."

"Oh, but there were several million Christians here years ago," Wang reasoned.

"I am sure they have all been reeducated by now," she said.

"It is true that they have received a brainwashing from the communists," Wang agreed. "But there are many who remain Christian."

"That's a lie!" she snapped, but she did not sound convinced.

"No," Wang told her. "It is a fact."

Cheetah took a deep breath. "These people have seen the great fruits of communism," she said emphatically. "They have been thoroughly taught. Why would they cling to such fables?"

Wang leaned forward. "Because," he said confidently, "they have a personal relationship with Jesus Christ. And when you know someone personally, it is very hard for anyone to convince you that he is a fable."

Cheetah's face reddened with anger. "Nonsense!" she exclaimed, a note of ridicule in her voice. "Show me this Jesus and I will admit that it is possible to know Him."

Lee had been sitting quietly and listening to their conversation, but now he spoke. "I would think you would be convinced by the effect He has on people," he said to her. "When I met Him, He changed my life. He transformed me."

Looking at him, she shook her head slowly from side to side. "You were a good student," she said sadly. "You had a grasp of theoretical concepts that was beyond even my comprehension. I cannot understand what happened to you. It must have been the prison."

"It was not the prison," he told her. "I met Christ. And

many young people right here in China are meeting Him today, just as I did."

She covered her ears with her hands. "No! I refuse to accept that!" she protested wildly. "Don't talk to me of such things."

"Fine," Lee agreed. "Let's talk about you. What are you doing?"

After a long pause she stated flatly, "I work in a factory. I am considered a refugee. I couldn't even get into the army."

Lee was amused at that, so much so that he found it impossible to suppress a caustic comment. "What a shame! All your talent and experience wasted!"

"Well, your training was not meant to prepare you for silly trips like this one," she countered, fixing him with an amber stare which gradually softened and became wistful. "We would have made a good team. Our organization would probably have been ready to topple the government by this time."

Lee, feeling uncomfortable, decided to channel the conversation into another direction.

"I have spent the past year as a student of theology in Hong Kong," he told her. "It is certainly different from working with Toto. But I feel I am still a revolutionary. Now I am trying to stir up a revolution in the hearts of men."

"But religion is dying out," she insisted. "Marx and Lenin agreed that during the dictatorship of the proletariat, religion would die out because the need for it would be gone."

"They may have been right about religion in general," Lee allowed. "But anyone who has visited communist countries around the world will agree that faith in Jesus Christ is increasing and not decreasing."

"That's why it is necessary for communist governments to try to ban the circulation of the Bible," Wang added. "Their fierce opposition to it is the greatest evidence of its impact."

"Of course they oppose it," she stated. "No responsible leader would allow what he knows will hurt his people to enter his country."

"The capitalists allow the teachings of Marx and Lenin to be read by their people," Lee reminded her.

"They are fools!" she snapped. "That's why they will fall."

"Perhaps," Lee replied, "it is because they are confident that truth will triumph. Perhaps they are so certain of that that they are willing to let people openly consider the various ways of life available to them."

Cheetah, by now, was visibly distraught. "You are speaking foolishness," she said. "I cannot understand what has happened to you, Lee. You look like the same person. In some ways I feel that I know you so well, but when you talk like this, you are a different person."

"The Lord can certainly change things—and people—when He steps into the picture," Wang observed to her chagrin.

"The Lord? Ha! You are the one who has messed everything up. I wish you had been killed in that wreck!" she spat viciously.

"Sorry you feel that way," Wang shrugged casually. But his calm attitude only seemed to anger Cheetah the more. She stood up and walked to the door.

"When I saw you two in the park, I decided then that I was going to have my revenge," she declared triumphantly. "My friend at the hotel desk tells me you are checking out tomorrow. That is why I came here tonight. I just want you to know that you will never leave China alive!" And having said that, she turned and left.

Lee breathed a sigh of relief, then said quietly, "She still rather overwhelms me."

"She is a bitter, unhappy woman," Wang replied, shaking his head hopelessly.

"I'm afraid she has a right to be," Lee said. "She has had a very hard life. I feel sorry for her."

"Do you?" Wang smiled. "I sometimes think you have deeper feelings for her than just sympathy."

"I have loved her and I have hated her," he said simply.

"Right now, I suppose sympathy mixed with fear would be the best description. She has reason to want to destroy me. What do you think she will do now?"

"No telling. She's bitter and frustrated. Back home she had worked her way up to being a key person in the communist organization. Here she is just another factory worker. I think she'd like to get something on us so she could get some notice from the local party committee." Wang paused, searching for the words to express his other thoughts about Cheetah. At last he continued. "And I think she is confused by her own emotions. It is evident, even to her, that you are more at peace with yourself than you have ever been. That can't help but impress her."

Lee shrugged and said, "I don't think she cares one way or the other about how I happen to feel."

"You are wrong, my friend," Wang pointed out to him. "She cares very much for you."

Lee laughed. "You're talking crazy."

"I think not," Wang answered. "It is one reason she's so frustrated. She thinks she wants revenge against me, but she cannot have it without hurting you as well."

Lee thought he knew Cheetah better than that. "Cheetah is capable of anything," he told Wang. "She could trump up a case against us. She would not hesitate to fabricate any evidence she needs. She is not a sentimental softie."

"Indeed she is capable of anything," Wang agreed. "She has already proven that. And she will no doubt try to fulfill her threat in one way or the other. But she is upset and confused, and that will make her less capable of accomplishing her goals."

Lee began to pace the floor nervously. "Actually, there is not too much she can do. The worst would be to kill us."

"I don't think she'd try that," Wang assured him.

"Perhaps not. But it is a possibility. Another one might be a trumped-up charge to get us thrown into prison."

Wang nodded thoughtfully. "That is more likely. But she

wants to make a reputation. It would have to be a foolproof case. She would not want to risk being exposed."

"I know Cheetah," Lee concluded, "and what she would really love is to catch us at something."

"But that won't be possible, because we have already done everything we were going to do," Wang said, speaking vaguely in order to confuse anyone who might be listening to their conversation with a bugging device. "I think her job keeps her tied down here in town. She probably couldn't follow us tomorrow. But even if she does, we are just going to see things and to look for Christians, exactly as we told her."

Lee nodded in agreement, adding, "But even if she does her worst, the Lord led us here and we can accept anything He has for us here."

"Amen!" Wang said with real conviction.

"Then let's forget about Cheetah," Lee said, "and let me tell you the wonderful story I heard only this evening."

It was very late when they finally stopped talking and went to sleep.

The next morning they left on the train for the long trip to Peking. Lee was concerned about Wang because he was tired from lack of necessary sleep and was still having pain. Lee encouraged his uncle to sleep as much as possible while on the trip, but the discomfort in Wang's back and his legs made sleep impossible.

They hadn't seen Cheetah as they left the hotel. They did not mention her, but she was much on Lee's mind. He hadn't thought about her in a long time. Now, as they rode along, he closed his eyes and the memories flooded back. The bitter ones somehow didn't seem quite so painful now, and he realized that his hatred was gone. He found himself pleasantly recalling the good times they had shared, and forgetting the bad ones.

Wang used his time to read and to carry on casual conversation with the other passengers. One man was particularly curious about their home country. After everyone else had left their compartment he continued to ask probing questions about life there.

"But do the farmers own their own land?" he asked.

"Some of them do," Wang told him. "Some of them live on land owned by others and pay part of their harvest to the landowner. Others ask God to help them raise extra fine crops so that they can save up money to buy their own land."

"And you say that God helps them?" he asked.

"Oh, yes," Wang replied. God always answers our requests. He does not always give us what we ask for because He sometimes knows it is not for our best, but He always takes care of us."

"It is my understanding," the man said earnestly, "that God is just somebody who has to do with death. I have heard that God has a good place for some people after they die. Do you believe that in your country?"

"Our belief is quite similar to that," Wang explained. "We believe that God's Son, a man named Jesus, provides the way to this good place. All those who trust Him can be sure they will go there."

"Amazing," the man exclaimed. "And very interesting, too." A serious look furrowed his brow and in his eyes there was the look of unmistakable intelligence. "I have always wondered what it is like to die. It is very hard to believe that death is the end of everything. Something deep inside says that is not true. But how do you repay this Jesus for His services? It must be very hard for poor people."

"Not at all," Wang assured him. "In fact, Jesus says it is easier for the poor than for the rich, because it is so hard for the rich to believe."

"Yes, I understand," he said. "Chairman Mao also has taught us that it is hard for the rich to know right teaching. But I don't believe I have ever read anything in Chairman Mao's writings about this Jesus."

"Probably not," Wang replied, slightly amused at the thought.

The man pondered that dilemma for a moment and then spoke. "Perhaps this Jesus never came to China. Is He Oriental?"

"He is Asian," Wang said. "He was born in the Middle East." The man nodded his understanding and Wang went on. "Have you never heard of Christianity?"

The man's eyes flashed. "Christianity? Oh, certainly. I am with the police, and it is our policy to oppose this counter-revolutionary, capitalist teaching ever since I became a member. We don't hear much about it anymore. I think it is being eliminated from the minds of our people. I cannot really recall very much about it now. But why do you ask?"

"I just wondered," Wang answered casually. "We have some Christians in our country."

"That is too bad," the man said sympathetically. "I think if I were in your country, I would prefer to be a friend of Jesus. I have enjoyed talking to you. I must get off here." He rose and started down the aisle toward the exit.

"Good-bye," Wang said. "When Jesus comes to your village, remember that He is a good friend." The man waved and got off the train.

Lee was almost speechless with surprise at Wang's temerity. "You are really getting bold, uncle," he said. "Publicly witnessing to a policeman!"

Wang started to laugh and suddenly stopped, and a thin smile froze on his face. "I—hate to tell you this," he muttered between clenched teeth. "But I am afraid I am not going to be able to get up."

"What is the matter?" Lee demanded, noticing the pale, drawn look on his uncle's face.

"The pain in my back. I've been afraid of this. It hurts like it used to," Wang gasped. "And when it's like this, I can't walk."

Lee looked around him in desperation. "What can I do?" he asked.

Wang had slid down to a prone position across the seats,

and beads of perspiration stood out on his upper lip. "Get—help," he groaned. "Get me—off the train and—into the hotel. I—must rest in bed—for a few days. Perhaps that—will help."

Suddenly the seriousness of the situation struck Lee with blinding clarity. He realized Wang had been holding on by sheer force of willpower and that now he couldn't make it any longer. Getting up, he went to find one of the train attendants and explained the situation to him. The man was very sympathetic and brought a simple analgesic medication to ease Wang's discomfort.

In Peking the attendant obtained a stretcher and several men to help carry the now semiconscious Wang from the train. A government car was secured and Lee and Wang were driven directly to their hotel.

When the hotel manager saw one of his guests being carried in on a stretcher, he became very concerned and immediately called a doctor who arrived in short order and examined Wang.

"His back is in serious condition," the doctor said. "He should be in traction. Irreparable damage may already have occurred. Further movement, in this condition, may result in permanent crippling."

"But we have to take the train back to Canton," Lee explained to the doctor.

"Imposssible. You must not attempt it. We will keep him quiet for a few days and treat him with acupuncture. Perhaps you could leave by plane after that."

Lee was almost frantic. "But we don't have permission to leave the country by plane," he protested.

"Perhaps I can help with that," the doctor said quietly. "The hotel manager will help you to contact the proper officials at the tourism office tomorrow. Your uncle will sleep through the night. I will come back in the morning and begin treatment."

Lee thanked the doctor and walked with him to the door. When he was at last alone, he sank to his knees beside the bed, his mind assailed by doubts and fears.

Why does the Lord allow things like this to happen? he asked himself. They had come here to serve Him, and Lee felt that He had let them down. Overcome by disappointment and helpless frustration, Lee continued to kneel there for a long time, waiting for an answer. Gradually his anger and frustration began to subside and he felt the peace of God filling his heart. He knew that God was still in control. Finally he went to bed and slept peacefully.

12 "My Dearest Sylvia . . . ."

The next morning Wang was still unconscious. The doctor arrived at about ten o'clock with an assistant, and together they began the acupuncture treatment.

Meanwhile, Lee began the complicated procedure of obtaining permission to leave China directly from Peking. Everyone he talked to was very courteous and helpful while informing him of the utter impossibility of such an endeavor. Travel plans in the People's Republic, he was told, had to be approved in advance. Furthermore, all entrances and exits had to be through Canton and by way of the Pearl River crossing. Frustrated and discouraged, he nevertheless went through the motions of filing his request in all the proper places before returning to the hotel. As he entered the room, he was startled and surprised to hear Wang's voice.

"Good day, my friend."

"Well, you certainly look much better than the last time I saw you," Lee said in surprise. "How are you feeling?"

"Much better than yesterday," Wang smiled as he shifted to a more comfortable position in the bed. "My back is still numb and my leg aches a little, but I feel much better. This

147

acupuncture is amazing. Yesterday I was almost afraid that your friend Cheetah's warning might be a prophetic one!''

Lee nodded in agreement. "The same thing occurred to me," he admitted. "It bothered me for a while, but then the Lord showed me that Satan is the author of fear. Last night it was very hard for me to see the hand of the Lord in this turn of events, but today I feel that He is still in control of the situation. Did the doctor tell you that he is going to try to help us change our travel arrangements so that we can fly out?''

Wang nodded. "He seems to feel that he can help eliminate much of the red tape. No pun intended.''

Lee smiled, enjoying his uncle's attempt at humor, then went on. "We can't fly directly to Hong Kong," he said. "We will have to go to Tokyo and then back from there. But it will be a lot easier on you than the train ride.''

"Do you think they are going to approve that?" Wang asked hesitantly.

"I must confess that I really do," Lee replied with enthusiasm. "Everyone says it is impossible, but I feel confident that the Lord is in this thing. If the doctor makes his report strong enough, that will do it.''

"His report is going to be very strong. He is convinced that my condition is serious," Wang assured him. "He says that it would be very bad publicity if the news got out to the effect that internal restrictions had caused me serious injury. He seems very sure that the authorities will want to get me out of the country as quickly and as directly as possible. And besides," he said, pausing for dramatic effect, "he is a chosen one!''

Lee's jaw dropped in amazement. "The doctor—" he said, stopping as Wang waved him to silence.

"He doesn't talk about it," Wang explained. "Perhaps you could get him to give you more details under other circumstances.''

"I'll try," Lee said quietly, lost in reflection. Indeed, he was beginning to see the hand of the Lord in this matter.

Later that same afternoon the doctor returned. He seemed very pleased with Wang's improvement and although he was pleasant he nevertheless retained his professional demeanor.

"I have turned in my report," he told them. "You will have to wait for the reply. You will need all the help you can get," he added significantly with a brief glance toward heaven.

As he prepared to leave, Lee moved with him toward the door. "I was just going out," he said casually. "May I accompany you, doctor?"

The doctor shrugged amiably and they walked out of the hotel to the busy street. The doctor retrieved his bicycle from its parking place and together they walked in silence to a side street. When they were sure they were alone, the doctor spoke.

"I assume that I was able to successfully communicate to your uncle that I, too, am a believer."

"Yes," Lee said. "He told me. But how did you know we are?"

"When we were taking his clothes off I noticed he was carrying some Scripture memory cards."

Lee was surprised. "But how did you recognize them? Are you that familiar with the Bible?"

The doctor shook his head. "I have never seen a Bible," he admitted. "But our teacher told us about putting Scripture verses on small pieces of paper in order to memorize them. It is very important for us to commit the Bible to memory."

"Where do you get the verses?"

"From the radio broadcasts, mostly. When the teacher is here he helps us."

"This teacher you mention—who is he?" Lee asked.

The doctor eyed him suspiciously. "We never tell that," he said.

Lee was quick to attempt to quiet the doctor's fears. "I don't need to know his name," he said reassuringly. "I just wonder how there can be such a teacher here."

The doctor leaned against the handlebars of his bicycle and

took a deep breath before answering in a quiet voice. "He is a man who goes from place to place and teaches people about the Lord. He has memorized several books of the New Testament. He is a great teacher." He spoke hesitantly, as though trying to determine just how much information to reveal. Then, at last, he changed the subject. "But what about you? What are you doing here?"

"My uncle and I came here specifically to aid other Christians," Lee told him. "We brought Bibles in with us to give away."

"Praise God!" the doctor exclaimed, a look of intense longing on his face. "I didn't know this could be done. Have you met many believers?"

"Oh, yes," Lee assured him. "Quite a few."

"That is wonderful. You would not happen to have one or two Bibles left?" he asked, his voice revealing a mixture of hope and fear.

Lee smiled. "Yes. We certainly do. We will gladly give them to you."

The doctor's eyes shone brightly with uncontained joy. "Praise God!" he whispered intensely, grasping Lee's hand.

"Tell me a little more about the teacher," Lee insisted. "How can he travel like that?"

"He is an old man and he travels only a short distance at a time. He has no job. He just goes from one group to another. The people feed and clothe him and he teaches them. He says that he is following the pattern of Saint Luke, chapter nine, except that he has no companion."

"Amazing!" Lee said. "I would not have imagined that there were such teachers. Is he the only one?"

"I know of two such people," the doctor told him. "There may be more. I do not know."

"Did he introduce you to the Savior?"

"Oh, no. He does not speak to unbelievers. It is up to the believers to do that. He must not endanger his ministry." The doctor paused, then explained, "I met Jesus through the radio broadcasts. I was stationed in the mountains several years ago and there I had a shortwave radio. I was looking for some good music late one night and just happened to stop with the dial on the Far East Broadcasting Company station from Manila. The program was very good. After that, I began to listen often. I found that deep inside I believed what they were saying, so I accepted Jesus as my Savior. For a long time I thought I was the only believer in China. Then last year the Lord led me to another one here in Peking, and he has brought me into their fellowship."

"How large is the fellowship?" Lee asked.

"We are seven adults."

"Do any of these people have Bibles?"

"No. As I told you, I have never seen one."

"God does provide! We have seven Bibles left, including the ones we have been reading ourselves. Since we will be flying out from here, we will not need them any longer. Your friends are most welcome to them," Lee said happily.

They had been walking slowly as they talked, and now the doctor stopped outside a large building and parked his bicycle. "I must make some calls here at the hospital," he said. "I will be back to see your uncle in the morning. I can pick up the Bibles then."

"Good-bye, doctor—and thank you," Lee said earnestly.

"Good-bye. Be very careful in the hotel," the doctor warned.

"I understand," Lee said. As the doctor walked into the hospital, Lee turned back toward the hotel.

There was no further opportunity for them to speak of these matters. Events occurred too rapidly. The officials not only permitted the exit by plane but required it as soon as possible, owing to the obvious improvement in Wang's condition. The doctor, however, was able to persuade them to allow Wang another day of rest before they were at last ushered unceremoniously to the airport and put aboard a plane to Tokyo.

Although the flight was brief, it was difficult for Wang to sit up. By the time they arrived in Tokyo he was in much pain and it was necessary for them to spend several days there in order to restore his strength before going on to Hong Kong. Lee had cabled ahead and they were met by David and Ruth with an ambulance at the airport in Hong Kong.

Wang was taken directly from the airport to the hospital. After he was settled comfortably in his room and resting quietly, Lee went with David and Ruth to a dinner at a nearby restaurant. There he eagerly shared with his friends the details of his trip.

"It's the Lord!" Brother David exclaimed again and again at each account of another believer encountered in the Mainland. So overjoyed was he at hearing of their success that he lost all interest in his food and continued to ply Lee with a rapid succession of questions concerning the trip. Ruth listened quietly, sharing their enthusiasm and rejoicing with them.

In the following days Lee and David spent much time together. David felt it was important that he gather all the information for future missions.

"But I am afraid to share names and addresses," Lee confessed to David. "What if you gave them to a spy by mistake?"

"Don't worry about that," David reassured him. "We don't give out names and addresses to anyone. We just keep them in order to keep track of people we contact. We need to know if more than one team makes contact with the same fellowship. Each new team that goes in must believe God will lead them to Christians, just as you did. However, you may give your contacts to a friend, if you want them to receive help before you can go back again."

Lee was glad to hear that. Before he could return to the Mainland, all of his contacts would need some kind of help.

"You do intend to go back," David presumed aloud.

"I hope to return," Lee said. After a moment's pause, he added, "But I'm not sure what to do about a certain communist on the inside who knows me."

David's eyebrows shot up. "How did that happen?" he asked.

Lee studied him carefully. "That's what I want to tell you about," he confessed. "It all started a long time ago—"

It was much later when Lee finally finished his story. He'd spared no detail, had told David everything. David had listened quietly, elbows resting on his knees and his big hands folded in front of him, staring at the floor. Occasionally he would glance up at Lee and nod quietly, urging him to go on. Not once did he register shock or surprise. When Lee was finished, David pursed his lips and shook his head thoughtfully for a few minutes while reviewing the details of Lee's story. At last he spoke.

"I would say that unless the Lord does something about that situation," he said regretfully, "you must not return."

Lee's heart sank. It was unthinkable that he would not return to China, for any reason! His whole life had been a preparation for this work. And what about the Christians on the Mainland who were counting on him, expecting to see him again?

"But, David," he protested weakly, not daring to look up. "I must return. Those people need help. Wang will probably never be able to make another trip."

David was considerate enough to pretend not to notice the emotion in Lee's voice. "What about Joshua Loo?" he suggested. "He is very interested in going. Would you trust him with your contacts?"

"Certainly, I would trust him," Lee said quickly. "But the point is that *I* want to go back."

"Then we must commit it to the Lord and seek the Lord's will," David said emphatically. "Let's pray right now."

As they prayed, Lee was suddenly aware that the same peace he'd felt before, there in the hotel in Peking when he'd thought God had let him down, was once again filling his heart. All at once he knew that God had the answer to this dilemma and would reveal it in His own good time.

"Things will work out," he said to David. "I feel the Lord is telling me just to wait."

"I believe they will, too, brother," David said. "Praise the Lord!"

It was three weeks later that the letter came. It was addressed to Lee Kai-chang and sent to the seminary, and it was mailed from the People's Republic of China.

Lee knew before opening it that it had to be from Cheetah. She was the only person in China who knew him by that name. The familiar feelings of fear and excitement that she always aroused in him welled up again, mixed with honest curiosity. Was there no escaping her, ever? What did she want now? He had to admit that she'd been on his mind much lately, and he had frequently prayed for her. In spite of himself, he knew that he would always care for her. He tore the envelope open with trembling fingers, half eager, half dreading the message inside.

"Dear Lee," it began. No sarcasm. Just "Dear Lee." *How unlike Cheetah,* he thought. He read on.

As you read this it is evident that you have arrived safely back in Hong Kong. I don't know how you did it. My friends here assured me that you would have to return this way.

I had an interesting reception here for you, but it didn't work out. [*You bet it didn't,* he thought. *Sorry, Cheetah—foiled again!*]

I am glad now. I am sure my hatred for myself would have been even greater after it was over. [Lee was amazed, and his heart was strangely warmed. He read on.]

I would like to know how you were able to arrange your return. Perhaps I have always underestimated you.

As I think back I must admit that in your quiet way you have found more success and happiness than I. And you did not take advantage of your parents' wealth to do it. That makes me think perhaps I could find some of that same happiness, if I knew how.

Please write to me. You have many good reasons to hate and distrust me. But I think you do not hate me. I hope you do not.

I have been thinking a lot about the people you said you were looking for here. If they are really here, as you said, they are a most amazing people. I must respect their courage.

You have known me as several different people. Please believe the real Sylvia is writing this letter. I will even do something you have never known me to do. I will ask for your help.

Hoping you care enough to write. Your servant, Chung Si-quo

Sitting at his desk in the dormitory, Lee bowed his head and thanked God for many answers to prayers, especially this one. He recalled how frequently of late he'd been tempted to doubt God. He confessed each instance and asked the Lord to forgive him. He remembered again the night in the hotel room in Peking when Wang had become ill. He recollected how he had questioned God's love in allowing that to happen, how he'd felt that God had let him down. He realized now that their very lives had been preserved by God's grace in allowing Wang's collapse.

"Forgive me, Lord," he prayed. "Help me to trust You always, in all things. Thank You, Father, for making it possible, through receiving this letter, to continue the work to which I am called."

Then he took out a sheet of his own personal stationery, affixed the date at the top of the page, and began: "My Dearest Sylvia . . . ."

Epilogue

The ministry to the suffering Church continues inside the People's Republic of China.

Many more Lees and Wangs and Joshuas are needed. They must be Chinese. They must have specific skills, such as language proficiency. Even more importantly, they must be mature Christians who are willing to accept 1 John 3:16 literally. "It is by this that we know what love is: that Christ laid down his life for us. And we in our turn are bound to lay down our lives for our brothers." (NEB)

Christians other than Chinese are not free of responsibility, however. When one part of the body suffers, the whole body feels the pain. The Church of Jesus Christ worldwide must weep with those who weep. And the Church must remember to pray for those who suffer persecution for the cause of Christ.

Everyone who shares the Lord's concern for these brethren is invited to join us as a prayer fellowship. These people will be kept informed of specific prayer requests.

Our Lord made it clear to Paul, as recorded in Acts 9:4, 5,

that when the Church suffers, He feels the pain. Do you share that suffering? Can you do less than lend your prayer support to those whom He has called into the fellowship of His suffering and who are risking their lives daily to serve Him in that calling?

Today couriers are traveling into China delivering God's Word to believers. For more information about the ministry to China, write to:

Open Doors with Brother Andrew
P.O. Box 2020
Orange, CA 92669